Anne...
all... your heart!

hush

AMANDA MAXLYN

Amanda Maxlyn
love

Editing provided by: Vasko Publishing
Cover design provided by: Amy Queau with Q Design

ISBN-13: 978-1542831017
ISBN-10: 1542831016

FOR SARAH.

Because we've all had a Mr. Lentz at one point in
our life.

TABLE OF CONTENTS

Chapter One

"I'm sorry it came to this. If you need a reference in the future, please let me know. I'd be happy to help you out in any way possible." My eyes follow the chapped lips before me as I try to comprehend the words that were just spit my way.

"I'm sorry, what?" I ask with confusion. I obviously didn't hear him right because there's no way my boss just fired me.

"If there is anything I can do, please let me know," he repeats, a little slower this time. Then adds, for the fifth time since we sat down together, "I'm sorry, Emma."

I open my mouth, but I quickly close it when no words flow out. I wait for the right letters to align together and register with my mouth, because right now all I can think of stammering out is, "What the fuck? Are you shitting me? It's my birthday! You're an asshole!"

Taking in a deep breath, I calmly recollect my thoughts. "But why?" I'm shocked at how soothing my voice is.

My now former boss, Mike, pushes away from the mahogany desk that looks just as old and tired as he does and shifts in his chair uncomfortably until his arms eventually end up crisscrossed in front of his chest. His eyes dart over my shoulder to the empty canvas on the wall, then slowly drag to the ugly eggnog carpet that covers his office floor. He clears his voice, avoiding eye contact. "Look, Emma, you're a nice young girl and I'm sure you'll succeed…"

"Just not here," I cut him off. Not that I see myself succeeding in the restaurant business as a waitress, but that's beside the point. I need a job.

I need *this* job.

Or rather, I need the tip money for living expenses.

I watch Mike close his eyes at the same time

he releases a heavy sigh. His shoulders drop and his body slouches forward in annoyance, or defeat. Maybe it's sympathy. I'm not sure.

"I'm sorry. I really am. You have to know that, Emma." His dark brown eyes shoot up now, making contact with my own. I can see the softness that lies behind them. "This isn't easy for me either. You're a great girl and I enjoy your presence. I've known your family a long time and want to help you, but from a business perceptive it isn't working out. You have to feel that too." Of course he feeds me the classic "it's not you, it's me" line.

"I had one bad week," I defend, holding up a single finger. As if that finger will back up my case.

"Um—more like a bad three months," he counters, slightly choking on his words.

I shrug with a small wave of my hand and an eye roll. "Who's counting?"

He looks annoyed now, his mouth forming a straight line, body relaxing and eyes drawing inward. I wait for him to fire back with something like, "I'm counting, obviously," but he doesn't. Instead, he's professional and polite as he continues: "I'll be more than happy to give you a reference if needed. I meant what I said. You're a nice girl, Emma, with a bright future, but maybe you'd be better off focusing on your swimming future without the distractions of rushing to a job that you'd rather skip and stay in the water for."

I can sense the caution behind his words as he watches for my reaction. Sure, I messed up a couple orders here and there, or forgot a soda every now and again, but what server in the food industry hasn't done that from time to time when first starting out? Does that really warrant for such drastic measures? I never claimed to be perfect.

I sit up taller, attempting to appear more confident than I feel. I give him my best fake *Bring It On* cheerleader smile before offering, "What about hosting? I could do that!" I can't mess up walking someone to their table.

When he drops his chin into his chest and closes his eyes in frustration I know this topic is not negotiable.

My fake smile fades and I give him a short, understanding nod, even though I know he can't see it. Holding out my hand, I say, "Thanks for everything, Mike. I may take you up on that reference. I appreciate everything you've done for me these last few months."

His head snaps upward and stares at my hand before him. When he doesn't take it, I give it a little shake, encouraging him to accept the gesture.

"Oh, right!" His eyes go bright with recognition as he quickly stands and takes my hand, grasping it tightly, followed by a small shake. All the tension in his body fades away when our hands break apart. "Sorry about all this. You take care, all right?"

I purse my lips. "Yeah, you too."

I get the feeling he's never fired anyone before, seeing how all this went down. But then again, I've never been fired before either, so I don't really know if there is a nice way to tell someone to take a hike. The hard part in all of this is that he's actually right. I'm a terrible waitress and would rather be in the pool than working, but it doesn't make getting fired any easier.

Mike stares at me, his feet shifting from side to side. It's like having an awkward breakup. You're not sure who should walk away first, have the last say, or if you should just laugh or cry at the entire situation.

When he doesn't make a move for the door, I do. I turn and walk out of the office, letting the door close softly behind me, not offering a final goodbye.

Treading quietly yet quickly, I dash through the customer-free dining room. Once the main doors come into view, my long legs move even faster and I do my best not to look at any of my former coworkers, who've now stopped what they're doing to watch me. I'm humiliated enough and don't need any compassion or judging eyes thrown my way. I don't know what's worse: doing the walk of shame after a one-night stand or the walk of shame from your boss's office after getting fired.

I'm sure both are equally mortifying.

Afraid of making any sound to draw more attention to myself, I hold my breath. I can feel the stares burrowing their way into my back as I push open the lobby door. Letting the mid-October sun hit my face, I tilt my head back, allowing my cheeks to soak in the damp air. My lungs release the warm breath of air I've been holding in so tightly. The light Florida humidity begins to melt away the tiny amount of numbness that has seeped inside of me.

The reality of the conversation that just took place consumes me as I stand in front of the large brick building, reading *Red's Cafe*.

"I just got fired," I confirm out loud to no one but myself, shaking my head in disbelief. I pick up a shift on my twentieth birthday and this is the thank you I get? "Happy fucking birthday to me," I mutter.

Once I'm behind the wheel of my 2007 Honda Civic with the windows down, I blast "Summertime Sadness" by Lana Del Rey. It's not summer, but the song is fitting for the situation. I make the short drive back to my newly rented townhouse that I'm sure I can no longer afford.

"Hey, you," my sister, Brooke, announces with surprise as she sets a moving box down on the living room floor. "What are you doing back so early? Did Mike decide to let you off for your birthday?"

"I got fired," I huff out, half pissed, half annoyed, as I toss the car keys on the center island that's still covered in newspaper from me unwrapping dishware almost two hours ago.

Her face falls. "What? Why?"

"What happened?" Ali, my sister's best friend and our roommate, asks with equal curiosity.

"I don't want to talk about it." I push the pile of throw blankets on our hazelnut brown microfiber couch to the floor and plop down, crossing my arms in frustration. I'm not upset at either for asking, but rather the entire situation in general. The three of us just signed this lease, and now I'm jobless. It's depressing.

Brooke calmly walks over and sits on top of the coffee table directly in front of me, resting her hands neatly in her lap. A pile of TV cords is tangled next to her. My nose bunches at the smell of Pine-Sol from her cleaning all day. Her long, thick sandy-blonde hair is piled high on top of her head in a messy bun, small baby hairs sticking straight up. She's wearing black yoga pants with a tight yellow sports bra showing off her petite, fit frame. Even with no makeup and dressed in some celebrity's workout line, she's extremely beautiful.

"Talk to me. What happened?" she urges.

"Apparently I make too many mistakes." *Like spilling a soda all over a customer's lap and then embarrassedly try to clean it up.*

Ali comes over and sinks in next to me. She wraps her arm around my shoulder and takes me into a gentle hug. "Oh, Em."

I've known Ali since I was ten and she moved in next door to Brooke and I. She's practically family, which is why I didn't hesitate to move into this townhouse with them.

"I see," Brooke says, responding to my too many mistakes comment. I can see the smirk on her face trying to peek through, but she does a good job pushing it away. Everyone knows I'm not the most nimble person. I can be a little clumsy at times.

"I see?" I laugh at her choice of words. "That's all you can come up with?" My head falls backward and my eyes fall shut, with the smile from my laughter still apparent. "I can't believe this is happening to me."

Ali lets go of my shoulders and taps my knee playfully. "Look on the bright side."

"What?" I pop one eye open to get a small glimpse at her exhausted, yet flawless face. I'm curious. Is there's a bright side to getting fired?

"Now you can help us unpack."

I giggle. It's a light laugh, but it still causes my stomach to tighten and my lips to spread wide.

I look around at the empty boxes spread out across the wood floors. "It looks like you two are managing just fine without me," I joke.

Ali laughs.

Bouncing up from the table, Brooke picks up the box she was once holding and walks into the kitchen that's off to our right, joining in on the laughter. "Honestly, Emma, it's not a big deal. So you got fired. We've all been there at least once in our life. It just took you a little longer than some to experience it."

"I didn't want to experience it," I mumble.

"It's not the end of the world."

Letting out a heavy sigh, I stand, leaving Ali to sit alone. The once unrecognizable living room is now transformed into an actual living space with everything perfectly placed in its rightful spot. Pictures are perfectly displayed on the fireplace mantel, artwork is hanging on the walls, curtains are up, and there's already a vibrant green plant in the corner.

"Not a big deal? How so?" I ask as I take my time walking toward her.

Her angelic eyes look me over. "You've worked your ass off since you were eleven, from babysitting to helping Mom and Dad to other odd jobs. You have more money in your savings account than men Ali has slept with, which is a lot."

"Hey!" Ali exclaims, standing up. She doesn't look offended, but rather amused.

Brooke smirks. "It sounded like a good analogy in my head."

I can't help but laugh.

"For real though, Em, take the semester off— or hell, the school year," Brooke says, bringing my attention back to her. "Your schooling is paid for with your full scholarship, along with a meal plan. You're too hard on yourself, always trying to take on too much at once. Think about how nice it would be to concentrate only on swimming for once."

I hate when she pulls the swim card out on me. Swimming is my life. It has been since I was three years old and my mom put me in a preschool swim class. "Ugh, I hate you sometimes." It would be nice to focus on swimming, but I know that's not possible.

"Never. It's impossible to hate a sister that's this awesome."

"While this little plan of yours sounds nice and all, you're forgetting the lease we just signed. I still have responsibilities with bills, and that meal plan you mention is only during certain hours." Brooke is correct when she says I have a good amount of money saved up, so *technically,* I could afford to take my sophomore semester off, however, growing up with parents who couldn't afford much really taught me the importance of saving, something my sister still lacks at her age.

She looks at me with proud, yet soft eyes. "Sometimes I forget I'm the older sister."

Brooke and I are complete opposites. She's more of a free-spirit, while I'm definitely a planner. Even with a six year age difference, we're very close.

"That's why I have to act like it sometimes," I tease.

"Ha-ha. Now go grab a box. The faster we

get this shit done the faster I can get out of here for my date, and you can go out with Ali for your birthday."

"Yes!" Ali chimes. "Come with me! It will be fun."

"I don't know. I think I rather stay in tonight."

"It's Friday," Ali states matter-of-factly.

"Your point?" I counter.

"You can't stay in on a Friday night. We *have* to go out!"

"Well, considering I've just been fired on my birthday, I was planning on locking myself in my bedroom, being depressed, drinking Brooke's expensive wine straight out of the bottle, polishing off a bag of jalapeno potato chips, and getting lost in ShondaLand."

Ali rolls her eyes.

Brooke giggles. "ShondaLand is Thursday nights, not Friday. Good try." She doesn't even mention the fact that I brought up the wine she's been saving for a special occasion.

"Ah-ha! *That's* the beautiful thing about Hulu. Every night is ShondaLand!" I give my best attempt at a finger point and wink, but fail miserably.

Ali and Brooke stare at me with the same "you've got to be kidding me" look.

"Maybe I'll read a book," I offer instead. Sometimes the road gets tough, but that's why Sylvia Day created men like Gideon Cross: so women like me can escape reality and pretend for a moment that our problems don't exist.

"You're not staying in on your birthday. I won't allow it. It was bad enough you were going to work." Ali cocks her head to the side, challenging me.

"I have to get up early tomorrow." I don't really, but it sounds like a good excuse to get out of whatever it is Ali is trying to drag me to.

"You don't have a job anymore to get up for," Brooke points out, looking over her shoulder as she walks into the pantry. *Thanks, Captain Obvious.* "Go have fun, Em. Then maybe you and I can go shopping this weekend sometime to celebrate your birthday."

"I have swim practice tomorrow!" I yell.

"At four," she calls back.

I've never hated Brooke knowing my schedule until this moment.

Ali bounces with glee, joining in on Brooke's quest to get me out. "When life hands you lemons, grab tequila, some salt, and drown your sorrows!"

A loud snort escapes from my throat. "I'm pretty sure that's not how it goes."

"Lemonade is too boring. Patron's more fun."

Grabbing the remote to the iPod dock, I turn up Ke$ha to block out their voices. Picking up a box labeled *Emma's Room,* I head up the small flight of stairs and close my door, locking myself in.

I'm thankful Brooke and Ali asked me to move in with them, getting me out of the dorms that smelled like stale beer and Bath and Body Works perfume, but I'm now wondering if this wasn't all a bad idea. They're both already in their careers while I'm still trying to figure out what I want to do with my life. Brooke is looking for Mr. Right while Ali is still playing the field, and

I'm just trying to pass exams and fit in swim practice. I think back to the dorm hall and how I at least fit in there, surrounded by girls I could relate to.

I need to find my new balance.

My gaze becomes glued on the empty white wall before me. I contemplate unpacking versus ignoring my problems for one night and going out.

Maybe spending the evening out won't be so bad.

Maybe it's exactly what I need.

Chapter Two

I tried to get out of the evening festivities, but after I finished unpacking the boxes in my room and Brooke left on her second date this week, Ali came barging in and wouldn't leave until I agreed to go to a masquerade-themed party for an early Halloween celebration.

"Remind me again how you know this person?" I ask, clasping together my diamond teardrop necklace that my parents gave me last year for taking first in the ACC championship and third in the NCAA Division 1 championship. They were so proud of me. It's not a big or flashy diamond, but it's perfect for me. A small water drop to keep close to my heart.

"A friend-of-a-friend kind of thing." She gives

a tiny shrug of her shoulders. "Apparently the mystery man your sister has been seeing told her about it, and she told me."

I squint. "So, what you're saying is we're crashing the party?"

She gives me a sly smile through the mirror in our Jack and Jill bathroom upstairs. This causes me to burst out in laughter. Figures we'd be going to a party that we weren't actually invited to.

"He told *her* about the party. She gave *me* the address. That's all the invite I need."

"Have you met him?" I ask.

Her ears perk up. "Who? Mystery man?

"Yeah." I apply a little bronzer to the hollows of my cheeks.

"No. You?"

"Nope."

"She must like this one," Ali says with a hint of laughter in her voice.

Brooke is a classic stage-five clinger. There are always instant fireworks after the first date. She doesn't waste any time bringing them home to meet the family and flaunting her puppy love in front of anyone who will take notice. Typically, by the second month she's already talking marriage, and that's usually when they run. But, she must *really* like this one if she has yet to bring him by in the six weeks they've been seeing each other. She hasn't told Ali or me anything about him, and dodges our questions when we try to get answers out of her.

"Okay, I'm all set." I watch as she finishes her last application of mascara and gives a small tug to the heart-shaped neckline that supports her two very noticeable assets. Her honey-gold hair is to the side, in a loose braid.

Ali has this aura that follows her. It's like a deep, exotic red bubble that calls upon men, and sometimes even women. They flock to her. And she's not shy about loving the attention it brings her. She's not vain by any means, but she most definitely loves it. For a woman in her mid-twenties, you'd think she'd be looking to find a nice man like my sister and settle down. But nope, not her. She'd rather play the field.

Glancing at my own reflection in the mirror, suddenly my simple choice of a black, knee-length Calvin Klein dress seems so boring compared to Ali's tight, red mini dress. My long, somber hair that fades from light brown to blonde is loosely curled, and my makeup is extremely light, except for my eyes. My eyes are vibrant shades of purple, silver, and a hint of brown, with black eyeliner and three coats of mascara.

"Don't," she says, as if she can read my mind. "You look great, birthday girl! Now, let's go celebrate." With those words she hands me a silver- and black-laced mask that only covers my eyes, and turns off the bathroom light.

When we arrive just after nine, the house is already packed. Bodies are scattered throughout the lawn holding red solo cups with

nothing but the glow of the moonlight above
them. The house is small, but charmingly nestled
quietly between a series of lady palm trees. It's
an admirable two-story blue-and-white house
with a wraparound porch and red door. Jack-o-
lanterns rest at the bottom of the steps with
cobwebs lining the posts, fluttering in the breeze.
Music swims through the speakers that are
swinging on an old wooden swing attached to
the porch. It feels like a heavenly secret escape.

 I securely tie my mask and give a quick once-
over in the rear-view mirror, my eyes popping
beneath the mask. Stepping out of Ali's older
model BMW, I head up the cracked porch steps
and enter the chatter-filled house, not waiting for
Ali to follow. The kitchen is just off the main
entrance, with bodies bumping shoulders inside.
Pumpkin-scented candles fill the air along with
hoots and hollers from already drunk guests.
There's a plethora of bottles to choose from
along with a keg by the sliding glass door that
leads back out to the porch. One of the best
things about going to a party where no one

knows you is they don't know you're not legally old enough to drink.

Ali comes up behind me. "I like your thinking," she exclaims, taking in the variety of rum, vodka, whisky, and wine bottles. Grabbing two cups from the large stack she starts pouring a small amount of Bacardi Limon. Not including a mixer, she hands me one of the cups. "Cheers," she says, and I watch as she slams back the liquid and pours herself another.

"Bottoms up," I say, and hold my cup up before slamming it back. It's sweet on my taste buds, but it burns my throat as I swallow.

After three shots, I mix in Sprite and sip on it. I've had a shitty day and could use more than a mask on my face to hide the embarrassment. Ali begins talking to a group of guys, so I sneak out the sliding door to the porch that opens up onto a large deck on the back of the house. There's a small group of people that have claimed a table-and-chair set. Lanterns give off light along with the flickering blue flame from the fire pit nestled in the corner.

The air is thick, but cooling off steadily, with the temperature sitting at a low seventy degrees, according to the temperature gage tied to a deck post. Tiny goose bumps claim my arms as I stare out into the darkness, resting my cup and purse on the sticky wooden railing next to me, the white paint chipping from being spilled on one too many times. I look out into the palm trees that line the yard. The sound of the waves is not too far off into the distance. Laughter slices through as a gentleman at the table behind me shouts a joke over the loud music. I can't help the smirk that slips through.

When I tuck my chin into my chest to shield the small breeze that sweeps in, out of the corner of my eye I see a shadow come up to my left. The body leans forward, resting both elbows on the same chipped railing. A beer bottle rests lightly between two large, smooth hands.

"You shouldn't hide your smile." His voice is soft, but has a small, smoky rasp to it. There's no roughness behind his words.

I turn my head slightly and look his way. My

smile slowly falters and fades. Next to me is a man. Even though he's leaning forward, I can tell he's tall. He's not some young college boy crashing a party. No, this is someone who's at least thirty, maybe even a little older. He's dressed very casually for this party, in jeans and a plain gray sweatshirt, with no mask. His brown hair is windblown, his face freshly shaven, and when he gives me a full-on grin I almost buckle at the knees. *Fuck.* He has dimples.

I stand up straighter and turn so my right side is against the rail. "It's getting a little chilly with the wind," I say in my defense. "It caught me by surprise." I give him a playful smirk, my cheeks shifting the mask up slightly.

He doesn't say anything. Instead, I watch as he stands tall and takes a long swig from his beer bottle. Contemplating his next move? I'm not sure, but I watch him with curious eyes. When he sets the bottle down, he removes his sweatshirt over his head. His undershirt slips up with it giving me a tiny glimpse of the lightly tan washboard abs underneath.

He holds it out for me to take. I look between his offering and his face. His golden-brown eyes are gentle. For a man, he has long, beautiful lashes.

"Take it," he says, waving it. Our fingertips lightly brush against one another, and I swear I hear him suck in a breath of air. His eyes almost look like they're in pain as his brows curve inward. His lips part as his gaze roams over my face and finally down to my body. Heat radiates throughout me. Suddenly I'm no longer cold. I hesitate slipping on his sweatshirt, but when I get a hint of his scent, I slip it over my dress and inhale the deep, woodsy scent. There's also a hint of apples mixed with a trace of after-shave and a bite of leather. I draw in another breath and let my eyes drift closed, letting the scent sink low in my lungs.

He lets out a small chuckle and my eyes pop open. He has his back against the deck rail and is watching me attentively with his head cocked to the side.

"Better?" He arches an eyebrow.

I nod, somehow unable to speak.

"Good." When I don't say anything further, he offers more. "I'm Trey."

Trey. I say his name in my head, getting a feel for it on my tongue. The name fits him. Masculine yet soft.

I don't offer up my name, which gets me another dimple-showing smile.

My heart flutters.

Trey's lips lift. "I haven't seen you here before. You a friend of Jill's?"

"I'm a friend of a friend." I use Ali's choice of words from earlier in the night.

He nods with an ever-growing grin. "All right, friend of a friend, what are you doing out here alone?"

I take a slow drink from my cup, trying to loosen the dryness in my throat.

"I'm not alone," I joke, pointing to the chatty table behind us.

Trey's eyes laugh with me. His lips part around the end of the bottle, but as he takes a long drink, I swear it's his eyes drinking *me* in.

Once he finishes his snail pace of a drink, he says, "Honestly, what are you doing out here hiding?"

"I'm not one for crowds tonight. I'm better off in the shadows."

"Somehow I doubt that. I'd spot you. A girl like you can't hide." He speaks with clear certainty.

My body flushes a deep shade of red.

I answer honestly: "I've had a bad day. I'm not really in the partying mood."

He takes another swig. "Cheers to that," he murmurs, lowering the bottle from his mouth.

I take another drink—not because I'm thirsty, but because I'm unsure what to say or do around him. He's absolutely breathtaking and I don't want to say something stupid and run him off.

"I was fired today." *Like that.* I'm not sure why I tell him that. I'm not looking for sympathy, and honestly, I'm not really that upset about the job any more. The more I think about it, the more I agree with Mike. It really wasn't a good fit.

"I broke up with my girlfriend tonight. Well…" He trails off, hesitating. His eyes scrunch together as he collects his thoughts. "I'm not really sure I'd call her my girlfriend, but regardless, she *was* the girl I was dating." *Ouch. Bad things really do travel in threes.*

"It's my birthday," I blurt. Not that this is a competition for who's having the shittiest day, but hey, if the shoe fits you might as well wear it.

"Shit," he exhales. "You win."

I giggle. "Sorry, I wasn't trying to compete with you."

He holds his hands up in defeat, smiling. "Can I get you another?" he asks, nodding to my now-empty cup. "From the sounds of it, we both could use another."

My body is already feeling light. From his company? The alcohol? Either way, I welcome it and accept another drink. "Please." I hand him the cup.

"What are you drinking?"

"Bacardi Limon and Sprite."

"One Bacardi, coming right up." He peers at

me intently. I can feel the sexual magnetism between us. Its strong power causes me to take a small step toward him.

Before the force can pull me any closer, he turns and walks away, leaving me panting for air. How can a man I've just met have such a strong effect over me?

I watch as he walks away from me and into the house. His jeans shape his body perfectly. Not too tight and nowhere near baggy. His ass looks perfect. I didn't come to this party looking for a hook-up, but there's something mysterious about him that I like.

As he saunters back toward me, I take him in from head to toe. *Holy hell he's attractive.* He's definitely tall, well over six feet, which is at least six inches taller than me. Big brown eyes with a hint of gold that shines through, sharp cheekbones, smooth, thick eyebrows, a concrete jaw, and Viking-like broad shoulders. Trey is not skinny, but rather built with thick muscle. His arms are perfectly defined, and I bet his legs are carved flawlessly underneath his jeans. Perfect body for a swimmer.

"Here we go." His hands are full with my cup tightly gripped in one hand, two beer bottles for him clasped between his fingers, the Bacardi Limon bottle tucked under his right arm and a small Sprite bottle peeking out under the other arm.

I give him a questioning look as I take the cup from him and help shuffle the other items free.

Settling in closer to me, he answers my unspoken question. "I figured tonight calls for a pick-me-up. It's not how you start your day, but how you finish it."

I like where this is heading. "I'd say you'd be correct, sir."

"Sir?" He laughs.

I blush and look away. Tucking my hair behind my ear, my fingers brush against the mask. It's then I remember I still have it on. I forgot it was there this entire time talking to him.

When I look back up, I'm met with him staring directly at me. It's too easy to get lost in his eyes.

I swallow.

He licks his lips and my eyes shift downward. I do the same and hear a tiny growl in the back of his throat. The sound is provoking. It makes me want to grab a hold of his green shirt and yank his head to me so our lips lock together, never coming up for air.

"I like the mask. I think it's sexy." His voice is low and raspy as he traces the lace with his pointer finger.

"You do?" My voice is anything but calm. It's an octave higher than normal, sounding nothing like me. My heart rate speeds up. I can feel my entire body pulsate with each thump.

He gives a slow nod as if he's giving my mouth the approval it wants to move in closer. There's an unspoken urgency that moves between us. I swear he's about to kiss me, but he doesn't make a move.

I inch closer to him, willing him to do the same. His scent consumes me.

A few beats pass by.

"Fuck it." One second I'm leaning against the railing and the next I'm being swept into Trey's

AMANDA MAXLYN

arms as he jerks me into him, brushing his lips to mine. It's the lightest of touches. It's like he's waiting for me to yank away. When I don't, he moves more eagerly. Our mouths open together and my tongue gently glides over his. His hand lands on my waist and tugs me in closer. Our tongues work impatiently with one another. I can't get enough. Just as I'm about to wrap my arms around his neck, a car alarm sounds from the front yard, startling us both. We break apart in one swift motion and just stare at one another, panting. The group behind us pauses at the sound, but soon carries on with their conversation, unaffected and unaware of our kissing.

"Sorry about that." His chest rises and falls as he tries to catch his breath. "I don't know what came over me."

My hands tremble as I run a finger along my numb lips. "No, don't be sorry. I liked it." *Liked it? That's all you can come up with?*

He flashes me his charming dimples, and I flush.

I step back, giving us both some much needed space. There's an awkward silence that lingers between us. He spins his beer bottle between his hands while I stare off into the distance. After what feels like five unspoken minutes, I decide to lighten the mood and change the subject, hopefully move past the awkwardness.

"So, Trey, tell me, how do you know Jill?" I have no idea who Jill is, but he mentioned her name earlier, so I can only assume she is the one who owns this house and is hosting the party.

He takes a long drink of his beer before answering. "We went to college together back in Michigan."

"Michigan?" I raise my eyebrows. "Who in the world leaves sunny Florida to go to college in cold Michigan?"

He chuckles, turning to face me. "That's where I'm from."

His phone beeps in his pocket, but he ignores it.

"Really?" I'm surprised. "What brings you to

Florida then?"

"Besides the warmth? Work. I was transferred here."

I nod as if I understand what it is he does for a living. I picture him working in a corporate office, sitting behind a big desk in front of a wall made up of windows. Something sophisticated where he's head of department.

"Sorry." His eyes go weak. "I didn't mean to bring that word up."

"It's okay. I wasn't really good at my job anyways."

"Somehow I doubt that."

His phone beeps again. When he doesn't move to grab it, it begins to ring.

"Do you need to get that?" I ask, motioning to his pocket. "It might be important."

He's unaffected by the noise. "Not at all. It can wait. Please, continue." And just like that he continues to give me all his attention.

I take another drink, trying to hide the fact that every time he speaks my body is about to crumble.

"It was time for a change anyways," I continue, with a light waving gesture.

"What kind of change?" He appears to be genuinely interested.

I'm still trying to figure that out. "I need to do something that I'm more passionate about. I don't want to work in a position that isn't true to who I am." It's the honest truth.

"What kind of work do you do?"

Shit. I think about it for a moment. Do I tell him I was a waitress? That would only open up the next conversation—my age, what I'm aspiring to be, and further dialogue that will only lead to our night ending much sooner than I want. And I don't want our night to end. There's no reason for him to know I'm barely out of my teens and in college, working toward a degree in business that I don't even want, but that my parents insist is a good backup plan to swimming. Not that they don't believe in my swimming. They both just don't understand how I can make a career out of swimming.

I decide to shift the conversation to avoid me

all together. "Let's not talk about work."

"Good call," he agrees.

The sound of heels clicking against the wood walking toward Trey and I fills the night air. My eyes shift from him to the woman walking toward us.

"Hey, I've been looking for you," Ali says with relief as she moves more quickly. Her eyes move between Trey and I, and her mouth lifts into the biggest smile, showing off her perfect white teeth.

"Good evening," Trey declares, holding out his hand. "I'm Trey. I've been holding up your friend here, sorry."

"Oh, don't be sorry." She takes his hand, but looks at me with an approving nod and a look that says *holy shit, woman, you did well.*

I give her a warning look, which only causes Trey to smile wider next to me.

"What's up?" I ask Ali, shooting daggers her way.

"I ran into an old friend," she pauses, giving a small head nod backward. Both Trey and I look over her shoulder to see a man waiting a few feet behind her, shifting back and forth on his feet. "Are you able to drive my car home, or..." Shifting her eyes between us, she suggests, "Find a ride home?"

"I'll give her a ride," Trey offers, looking directly at Ali, with not as much as a sideways glance my way.

"You will?" I try my best to keep my voice steady and calm, but secretly I'm jumping with glee inside.

"Of course." It's with those words he shifts back to me. "I'll stop drinking now." With one intensifying look, he's able to make me feel as if I'm the only person that matters in this very second. There's no Ali, no group of people behind us, no party taking place. It's just him and me.

"Great! That's settled then. I'll see you tomorrow?"

"See you tomorrow." I don't look at Ali when I answer. My eyes stay zoomed in on Trey.

She says something else, possibly a goodbye

to Trey, but I can't be sure. The sound of her walking away is my only indication she left.

"I'm going to grab a bottle of water quick. Don't go anywhere." There's laughter in his voice. He doesn't give me time to reply. He swiftly turns and jogs into the house. Before I can get in a decent thought he's walking back toward me.

I struggle with taking my eyes away from Trey. When I try, he draws me back in, like a current sweeping out to sea, never to return.

There's a gentle breeze that moves through my hair, a small strand sweeping across my eyes and hooking onto my mask. Without hesitation Trey steps inward and tucks it back in place behind my ear. His fingertips barely come in contact with my skin, yet it's enough to cause my cheeks to flush and send my body floating off into space.

I know he feels the connection too, because he doesn't avert his eyes from me. His gaze burrows, looking straight through me and reading every emotion my body is feeling: Lust, desire, need. His hand eventually finds comfort at my waist, and he doesn't try to remove it.

"Tell me, Jane Doe, what are you into?" Trey's voice is barely a whisper. He asks the question with so much interest and yearning to know everything about me.

"I swim."

As soon as the words fall from my lips, he steps back, giving us space.

"Swim?" His eyes go wide in surprise. I watch his hand reach for the railing, finding a sense of balance.

I nod. "I love to swim. It's the first thing I think about when I wake up and the last thing before I go to bed. I'm my happiest when I'm in the water."

He opens his water bottle and takes a few big gulps.

I bite my lip as I watch him set it down and rub the back of his neck. When he looks at me, his eyes are bigger than before. He takes a few deep breaths, and I grow impatient for him to say something.

His finger lightly glides down my face. I feel like a breathless sixteen year old girl who is about to have her first kiss.

"You..." He falters. "You are simply the most intoxicating person I have ever met, yet I don't even know your last name."

My heart sinks to the pit of my stomach. I have no idea what made him say that, but hearing those words, and how genuine they sounded coming out, makes me want to know everything about him.

"I feel like you're asking all the questions tonight. How about you tell *me* something about yourself. What do you do for fun?"

My question gets me a boyish grin from him. "Well, since arriving here, I've taken quite a liking to the ocean and am now learning how to surf."

My eyebrows raise. "Really?" *That explains the tan abs.*

He nods. "I, too, enjoy being in the water."

"Is that so?" I smirk. *Dear God, I want this one.* I give a silent prayer.

I want him to elaborate more on the

swimming, but he doesn't. "I also like to read and enjoy a good movie," he adds.

Could this man get any more perfect? "Like what?" I try to calm my beating heart by playing with the fabric of my dress.

He chuckles, leaning back against the railing. His eyes look up into the night sky, his mind going deep into thought. "Oh, let's see. My favorite movie is *Sweet Home Alabama*, but if any of my male friends ever ask, it's *Gladiator*. I don't want to lose my man card."

I laugh so loud that I actually snort. His eyes dance with mine. "*Sweet Home Alabama?* For real?"

"What can I say? I have a thing for blondes." He gives me a wink and all the air leaves my body. I *have* to see this man again. "Would you believe me if I said I've read every Jane Austen book?"

I nod because somehow I believe it. "Now that I've heard what your favorite movie is, there is no reason for me to doubt you." There's a hint of amusement in my voice.

He leans in, his lips brushing against my ear. The faint smell of beer on his breath lingers between us. "If any of my friends ask, I'm a James Patterson fanatic. I do like him, too."

Trey makes me laugh until my stomach hurts and my cheeks want to burst from smiling too hard.

"I'm beginning to think your friends don't know the real you."

He swallows. "But you do." His voice is low. The small rasp from earlier in the night is back.

I can't help the jagged, painful thoughts that wash over me for not being fully honest about my age or that I'm still in college. A part of me feels dishonest, but I don't want this moment to end. Whatever this is.

I take a deep breath, pushing away the contemplation. "You've made the friend comment twice now. Are you planning on me meeting your friends?"

"Absolutely." He beams. It reminds me of Mr. Big in *Sex and the City* when he tells Carrie he believes in love at the end of season one.

Just after one in the morning he offers to take me home. I'm a little reluctant to end our night, but I give in. If I didn't already think he was a gentleman, he confirms it when he takes my hand and leads the way to his silver SUV parked out front. Once I'm settled in the passenger seat with the smell of leather all around me, I watch him cross the front of his vehicle to the driver'-side door. I lift the neckline of his sweatshirt up to my nose and inhale, trying to soak in as much of his scent as I can. I know the second I get home I'll need to take it off and give it back, and I want to remember this moment.

When Trey starts the engine, he doesn't move. His hands grip the wheel tightly, giving him a case of white-knuckle syndrome. Looking over at me, his eyes appear dark and weary. It's a look that pleads for me to say something to stop him from taking me home.

"Where to?" he asks. His eyebrows crease with disappointment, but his voice sounds hopeful.

"Your place," I murmur.

Chapter Three

Trey studies me. The gold in his eyes burns through me, sweeping out every deep desire within me. I sink back into the leather seat as my heart pulsates in anticipation. He peels his white knuckles from the steering wheel, and I hold my breath as I patiently wait. His breathing becomes labored as his lips part, and he leans over the center console so we're nose to nose.

"Is that what you want?" His voice is soft, barely a whisper. His breath is warm as it lightly hits my lips.

"Yes." I say the word with confidence. Not too quiet, not too loud. Now that we've come this far, there's no going back.

I lean in closer, willing him to claim my lips

once again.

But he doesn't. He scans my still-masked face and then down the curve of my neck. My dress has shifted up, resting just above the knee. I move to pluck it down, but his hands quickly find mine, stopping me, our eyes locked.

"Don't hide yourself from me," he orders. His gaze slides down my body, claiming me.

Ever so gently and with the lightest of touches, his finger glides across my knee and up my leg, igniting the burning ache between my thighs.

"Trey." I rush out his name with sudden urgency. His touch burns my skin. My eyes drift closed as I soak in his caress.

Just as quickly as he touched me, he backs away. My eyes pop open at the sound of his door opening and closing.

"Trey?" I sit up taller, reaching for the door handle. I'm not sure what I plan on doing. Run after him?

He stops at my door and opens it. "Come on."

I take his offering hand. His grip is strong, dominant. He leads me across the freshly trimmed lawn. The lady palm trees dance in the wind as we walk by.

"Where are we going?"

He doesn't answer me. His pace quickens, and I do my best to keep up, tightening my grip around his hand as we reenter the house and cross the living room to the staircase that's in the back right corner. No one pays us any attention as we swiftly move past them. We take the stairs one by one, a small creak beneath our feet as we go.

Upstairs it's soundless, like we've just been transported to our very own secret hideaway. We stop in front of a closed door at the end of the vacant hallway. Trey doesn't stop to knock or wait and listen if anyone is already occupying the opposite side. He enters confidently. Once we're locked away inside, he finally releases me.

There's a double-sized bed next to an open window that's letting in the midnight breeze. A small desk rests in the corner with a laptop, lamp, a James Patterson novel, three different swim magazines, and a large stack of manila folders. To my left is an open archway with a huge walk-in closet that opens into a bathroom.

I walk over to the window, tracing the bed with my hand as I do. The fabric is soft beneath my fingertips. The room smells of him.

"Do you live here?" I ask, looking out the window and into the backyard.

"Yes."

I whip around, my eyes wide in surprise. "Oh."

He takes a step forward, the moonlight illuminating his face as he walks toward me.

His left hand finds comfort at my waist as his right hand glides up my side and rests at the base of my neck, his fingers brushing along my collarbone. My eyes close and my head drifts to the side, exposing my neck to him. I can feel his warm breath just below my ear. His lips barely touch my skin. When his lips press more firmly I become lightheaded. My pulse quickens. I know he can sense the effect he has on me because I feel his lips turn upward against my flushed skin.

I moan the second his lips slide further up to my jaw. When he brushes my chin, just below my bottom lip, I lose all self-control. Trey begins to breathe heavily when my hands move to grip his face. Tilting my chin up, I move to lock our lips together. He teases me by backing away a little with a small laugh. My grip tightens and I stretch him back toward me.

He flashes me his dimples just before I crash my mouth to his. My fingers ache as I hold him close, our lips moving effortlessly together. I pick up the pace, my lips moving more hungrily. The urge to touch him everywhere consumes me as we pick up the pace and kiss more frantically. We both can't seem to get enough. His fingers press firmly into my side, leaving his mark.

His hands move to the hem of his sweatshirt and gently tug it upward. I help him, sliding it up and over my head. I can't seem to get it off fast enough.

Trey's fingers coast under my chin, down my neck and my side, across my back and upward, landing on the zipper of my dress. Tiny needle pricks cover my back with his touch. My knees feel weak as my breathing becomes labored.

I gather my hair and bring it over my shoulder, giving him the access he needs. He tugs downward on the zipper. "We need you out of this. Right. Now." He sinks into the crook of my neck, clasping his mouth onto my skin, devouring me. I shimmy out of my dress and let it fall to my ankles. My strappy sandals follow. Trey kicks them both across the room. A loud bang erupts from the sandals making contact with the wall.

I moan as he gives my shoulder a gentle bite. "Trey."

"Say my name again," he commands.

"Trey," I whimper, relaxing into his body.

His nips and sucks cover every inch of my neck. His tongue comes out and traces my earlobe, sucking it into his mouth and biting down. His touch is enthralling.

My hands tug on his T-shirt. I need to feel his bare skin against mine. He withdraws just enough to take his shirt off. Our mouths reconnect once his shirt falls to the floor. My body quakes with pleasure. He kisses me hard, almost to the point of pain. There's nothing slow or soft about this. Trey owns me and he sure as hell is letting me know it.

"I want you so fucking bad right now," he moans into my mouth.

"Take me to bed, Trey," I order.

In one motion, Trey scoops me up behind the knees, causing me to squeal out. This gets me a deep, throaty laugh from him.

He takes me to the bed, lays me down, and climbs on top of me, straddling my body. I grab his arm and tug him down playfully.

I welcome the pressure of his body as my legs spread open and he nestles between them. Before I can say anything, he reconnects our mouths. His tongue traces my bottom lip. My hands explore his chest, running my fingers up and down against his rippled stomach.

"Take this off," I beg, tugging on his pant zipper. There's a burning throb between my legs as his erection presses into me. "I need you inside of me," I plead into his mouth, as he sucks on my bottom lip.

"Fuck," he groans.

My lips become numb as he kisses me more forcefully. My hips thrust into him, begging for his touch.

He breaks our kiss. "Like this," he purrs against my ear, just as his finger pushes my wet lace underwear to the side and plunges them inside of me.

"Yes," I gasp at the sudden impact. My back arches off the mattress, needing him deeper.

His left hand slides down my chest, setting every inch of my insides on fire. He cups my breast and squeezes hard before sliding the cup of my bra down. He latches his fingers onto my erect nipple, pinching.

I moan out in pleasure.

His fingers never break from gliding in and out of me. "You feel so good," he growls breathlessly.

"I want all of you," I whimper, moving my hips at the same pace as his fingers. My vision becomes clouded with pure lust for him. My body never craved for anything more.

"And I want to see all of you." His fingers slow their pace inside of me. I feel like I'm about to combust under his touch. He sits back on his heels and I cry out at the loss of contact from his fingers. His eyes engulf me.

Hooking his hands under my back, he unclasps my bra and tosses it to the floor. Leaning forward, he sucks one of my nipples into his mouth, and I whimper. His hands rest at the top of my underwear and he begins to rip them down. My hips rise, helping him slide them down my legs.

Once I'm bare before him, he gets off the edge of the bed and yanks my ankles so my body is at the end of the bed. I rest up on my elbows watching him get on his knees and rest before me.

"You're so beautiful. I want to fuck you with my tongue."

Holy shit. My knees tremble.

I fall back, sinking into the mattress, letting his scent consume me. My eyes shut as a cool rush of air hits my clit. I wait for his contact, my lips parting in expectancy.

The second the tip of his tongue makes contact, I grip the sheets, balling my hands into fists. His tongue swirls around the swollen bud of my clit and down, sliding inside of me.

"You taste so fucking good," he groans.

I can feel my face burning. I run my hands up my body and into my hair. I forgot about the mask and I quickly untie it, throwing it somewhere across the room.

"Trey?"

"Hmm?" he hums against me.

"Don't stop," I beg.

His hands part my thighs wider, exposing me even more. The pressure builds deep inside as my hips rock against his mouth. My body liquefied beneath him.

"Go for it," he encourages. He slides his fingers inside of me and sucks on my clit at the same time.

My insides welcome his fingers and my body shudders. My body quivers beneath his touch, electricity jolting through me. His pace slows as my body comes to a rest. His lips press against the inside of my thigh, and he kisses me softly. His gesture more tender and comforting.

He shifts onto the bed and slides back up my body, planting a kiss on my lips. I smile as his body shifts above me. My eyes are heavy, and I have to will them open, still foggy from my orgasm. When I look up at Trey, my smile quickly vanishes.

His body is frozen above me. Trey's eyes have become wide and vacant. They're motionless. His face looks ill, like he's suddenly become sick at the sight of me. He blinks once, then twice.

My heart thumps inside my chest. I try to rest on my elbows, but the pressure of his body on top of me makes it difficult to move.

I brush my hand along his cheek, trying to bring him back to me, but his head quickly turns to the side. My hand drops to the bed.

"Trey?" I say, hesitating. I search his face, concerned. When he doesn't answer, I say his name again.

His head shakes back and forth, and I frown.

"Emma?" When my name falls from his lips,

my heart plummets to the pit of my stomach. All heat from my body is gone and shivers take over. The wind has just been knocked out of me.

"H-how?" I struggle to find the words.

He quickly pushes himself off the bed, putting a good distance between us.

"Shit," he spits. He runs his hands through his hair and begins to pace in a small circle, his eyes to the floor.

"Trey?" I scoot to the top of the bed, bringing my knees inward and grabbing his thick blue comforter to wrap around my now cold body. I'm not sure what the hell just happened, but no matter how many times I say his name he refuses to look at me. When he tries, he quickly averts his eyes. He acts like the sight of me disgusts him.

He rubs his neck raw, continuing to mumble to himself. I can't make out what he's saying besides a few *fucks* and *shits*.

I watch, unmoved, as he rapidly grabs his shirt and yanks it over his head.

When the door slams shut, I'm left alone, naked and suddenly feeling claustrophobic within the walls of his large room.

Chapter Four

My eyes gloss over from the humiliation I just endured. *Do not cry. Do not cry.* I continue to stare at the closed door, stunned. The door frame blurs in and out. I try to push my tears back.

The room no longer feels warm and inviting, like when I first entered. My bottom lip quivers so I quickly bite down, stopping it. *I will not cry.*

This is so out of character for me. I'm the girl that stays busy with school and work, dedicated to my swimming future. I don't get involved with guys like my sister or Ali. And I'm definitely not the girl that hooks up with a random guy the first night she meets him, but of course the one night I let my guard down for a pick-me-up, I run him off.

Figures.

I sink down into the bed. A light shiver moves through me.

"How the hell did he know my name?" I ask myself bewilderedly. I never once offered it to him, enjoying the mystery between us at first. I've never seen Trey before tonight, and him rushing away from me only confuses me more. I run the memory of his face through my mind, trying to place where I might have seen him before, but nothing comes. A man like him stays with you.

Tugging the covers over my head, I let out a muffled scream in frustration, followed by a sigh. I lie in his bed for another beat and then throw the covers off me and to the floor. Moving hastily, I get dressed and locate my purse to take out my phone. Seeing as Trey offered to take me home, Ali didn't leave me her car keys, so I'm now stranded. I call my sister as I take the steps down to the now quiet living room. When Brooke doesn't answer, I try Ali, but it goes straight to voicemail. Once I reach the bottom step I scan the room. It's not that I expect to see Trey standing there in all his gloriousness, but I can't help but look for his tall stature. I'm not sure what I'm hoping to achieve by looking for him. Yell at him? Slap him? Make him tell me how he knows me? Run my hands through his hair and kiss his soft lips? Demand he takes me back up into his bedroom and fuck me? Shaking my head, I head toward the front door and dial Brooke's number one more time.

Again, no answer.

Trey's SUV is still parked out front, so I know he's here somewhere. The temperature is certainly cooler and I wish I brought a light jacket tonight, or at least grabbed Trey's sweatshirt off his floor before leaving his room. I walk to the porch and to the back deck to see if I by chance recognize anyone. I know I won't, but I still check. I do a full circle, wondering if Trey will come out from the shadows and explain this entire fucked up *Twilight Zone* episode to me.

But he doesn't.

Taking a deep breath, I hold my pride and head back inside, hoping to find at least one sober person to give me a ride home, or at least the address to this place so I can call a cab.

I wake up to light peeking through my drawn shades. I rub the sleep from my eyes, hoping to wipe away the memories of last night and the image of Trey. When I got home in the early hours, Ali's bedroom door was open with her bed empty. Brooke's door was closed, so I assumed she had company, or was still out.

Once my eyes can see clearly, I locate my phone on the nightstand. *2:06 p.m.* Shit. I slept all afternoon and have swim practice at four. With our coach out on maternity leave sooner than expected, the assistant coach offered to run a special swim practice before the new coach's start day on Monday.

In the shower, I let the hot water run down my body, and I begin to scrub away the embarrassment of last night. Images of Trey's face cloud my thoughts. I'm sucked right back into recollections of our evening together. The way his lips took my nipple into his mouth, his feather-like touch setting my skin on fire, his tongue flicking against my clit and my body quaking around his fingers.

I lick my swollen lips and close my eyes at the thought of Trey sucking them.

My face flushes under the stream. How can one man make me so mad for leaving me stranded, yet, at the same time, the simple thought of him kissing and touching me makes me want to touch myself?

Running my hands down my thighs, I can still feel the marks he left on my body. A light moan slips out and my eyes pop back open. I splash the water over my face, letting it wash away the memories. Maybe this was all for the best? There's no room for romance with my busy schedule. With love comes complications. I don't need any more complications in my life. I admit the truth graciously. It doesn't matter how Trey knows who I am. What matters now is that I won't ever see him again.

Once I'm dressed and have my swim bag packed, I take the steps two at a time downstairs to find Brooke standing in the kitchen holding an empty cookie sheet with an oven mitt, with Ali sitting at the center island. The tall vase I unpacked yesterday is now filled with fresh flowers, a candle is lit on the stove, and the entire main living space smells of chocolate and cookie dough.

"You're baking?" I ask, stunned.

Brooke flashes me a smile, but it doesn't reach her eyes. She looks like she didn't sleep well, with dark circles under her eyes. Her hair is neatly brushed, but her face is cold.

"Is everything okay?"

She nods and flashes me the biggest "I'm lying" smile.

"Brooke," I say, encouraging her to answer me, but she doesn't.

"What are you doing here?" Ali swings her body on the stool so she's facing me. "I honestly didn't think you were home."

I roll my eyes. "Wow, thanks. Good to know I'm easy to forget."

She laughs, reaching a hand out to me. "No, no. That's not what I meant. I just figured how I left you last night, and not seeing you this morning, that you were *out*." She wiggles her eyebrows as she drags out the word.

Brooke looks between us. Suddenly her demeanor changes from somber to curious. "What are you talking about? How did you leave her?"

I walk over to the cookies that are cooling off on the counter and take a bite of one. "Since when do you bake?" I ask, holding the cookie up, examining it. It looks like a real cookie and tastes pretty amazing, too.

Brooke rolls her eyes and laughs.

"Don't change the subject," Ali warns.

Sighing, I lean forward so my elbows are on the counter. "I had the most intense orgasm of my life, and then..." I trail off, waving the cookie in the air.

"And then..." Ali nudges.

"You hooked up with a guy?" Brooke blurts out.

I shrug. It's half true. We didn't go all the way, but I don't feel like explaining myself right now. Regardless, I'm certain she's about to fall over in surprise.

"I knew it!" Ali shrieks.

"So, tell us. Who was it? How was it? Are you going to see him again?" Brooke spits out a million questions.

I stand up and head to the fridge. Grabbing a water bottle, I take a sip to coat my dry throat. I contemplate my next thought. They're both waiting patiently for me to continue, ears perked, eyes lit, grinning in a way that look like it may hurt. I'm about to continue with the story and tell them all about how he knew my name and then ran off with me still naked in his bed, but I refrain from telling them any of it. I don't do this. I don't sit around and talk boys with my sister and Ali. I've had boyfriends, yes, but I'm not one to kiss and tell, and considering they both know I don't really do the hook-up thing, they're even more intrigued about my sex life in this very moment. Seeing them both sitting in front of me, hanging onto my every move, the last thing I want is for them to take more pity on me after the day I had yesterday once they find out what happened last night. So I don't tell them. Instead, I say, "He was just a random guy at the party—a friend of a friend, passing through town. I won't be seeing him again."

It's not a lie. He's some random guy from Michigan, and I won't be seeing him again. Trey made that clear.

Ali's face falls. "Not you too?"

I raise an eyebrow. "Me too?"

"First your sister, now you."

I look over at Brooke, who adds another baking sheet to the oven. "I told you, Ali, it will all work out." When she looks at me, she gives me a "don't worry about it" smile and shrugs.

"What's going on?" I look between Ali and Brooke.

Brooke sighs. "Ali is just exaggerating."

71

"No, I'm not," she interrupts. "The man broke up with you, Brooke, and you're over here baking cookies for him!"

I whip my head around to Brooke. "What?"

Brooke clears her throat. "The night started off great. We were laughing in the car and he even held my hand walking into my favorite Mexican restaurant. He was super sweet, but then, the next thing I know, he's telling me he wants to take some time apart. Things were apparently moving too fast for him."

I look at the two-dozen cookies cooling off in front of me. "So you're making him break-up cookies?"

Ali snickers.

"No, smart ass. I invited him over."

I tilt my head to the side. "I'm confused. If he broke up with you, why is he coming over?"

"Because I texted and called him until he agreed to come over and talk." *Yup, stage-five clinger.*

Ali leans over the counter and grabs a cookie. "I'm glad you're awake, Em. Now you get to sit with me, eat these warm cookies, and watch the show play out. Best part, it's live. That's even better than some recorded ShondaLand show you have saved."

"Very funny, Ali." Brooke purses her lips. "I know I've broken all the rules, but I was so confused last night. I still am! He didn't give me time to digest it at the restaurant. I tried to text and call when I got home, but he didn't answer. He called me back this morning and said he *really* needed to talk to me. I think he's going to tell me he made a mistake." She sounds hopeful. My poor, clueless sister.

"Or he wants a restraining order," Ali offers as an alternative.

Brooke mumbles something and I take that as my cue to leave.

"Well, ladies, while this is all wildly entertaining, I'm off to swim practice."

Ali grabs another cookie and heads up to her room. "Don't start the show, Brooke, until I come back!"

Brooke sighs.

Just as I slip my swim bag over my shoulder, there's a knock at the door.

"That's him!" Brooke practically jumps out of her chair. "I'll get it."

It's too late. I swing the door open and right there, standing before me in a ball cap, jeans, and a T-shirt, is Trey. Just like last night, I'm sucked in, unable to look anywhere else but at him.

Holy shit.

"Trey?" I choke on his name. *Is this real?*

Trey grabs a hold of the door frame, steadying himself. His eyes look like they're about to fall out of his skull. But his lips look just as soft as last night, and I'm not sure if I want to push him against the wall and salvage them or smack them right off his face for last night.

"Emma," he breathes.

"Trey! Thanks for coming over," Brooke beams as she comes to stand next to me. "Trey, I'd like you to meet Emma, my sister. Em, I'd like you to meet the new swim coach."

Oh, fuck.

74

Chapter Five

"I'm sorry, but do you two already know each other?" Brooke's words fracture my thoughts and bring me back to Earth. She's moving her head back and forth between us, pointing.

Trey's eyes are unmoving. Mine narrow in.

Trey clears his throat, offering me a smile. "No, I don't believe we've met." He holds his hand out. "I'm Trey Evans. It's nice to meet you."

Evans. The last name fits him, too. I guess I was wrong for placing him in the corporate world.

I look over at Brooke then Trey. I can't think. *This* is the guy Brooke has been dating? *She's* the girl he broke up with last night? My head is foggy. My eyes bounce from his hand to his face.

"Emma?" Brooke nudges. I look at her and see she's motioning to Trey's hand.

I don't take it.

Brooke sways next to me, and lets out a heavy sigh. "Emma, Trey is a transfer from Michigan to fill the new head coach position while Coach Stephens is out on leave. He was the assistant coach at a university back in Michigan."

My eyes water and I'm ashamed for either of them to see. I pass my tears off as frustration toward my sister. "So, you're what? Dating the faculty now?"

I'm hurt, embarrassed and frustrated at this entire situation.

"I didn't want you two to meet like this, Em." Her voice is soft.

My breathing picks up and my head spins as I try to piece this all together. When it rains, it pours.

I look back up at Trey. *Coach Evans.* It's all starting to make sense. The way he acted when he found out I was a swimmer, him telling me he liked the water, too, and the three swim magazines on his desk. There's no way I could have known he was a coach, but small signs were present. I should have asked more questions.

"We met this summer when he came for a tour. I took him out. We stayed in touch, and when he moved here we started dating. I didn't want things to become uncomfortable between you and me, with him being the new head swim coach, so I didn't tell you or Ali about it." Brooke's comforting voice sounds just like our mother's when she's trying to cheer one of us up.

"Emma." Trey takes a cautious step forward, his hands slightly raised in a defensive stance. His shoulders slump forward when I back away abruptly.

I put a hand up, stopping him. "*Coach Evans,*" I hiss. "While I'd love to stay and chat and watch you rekindle your romance with my *sister,* I have a swim team that's waiting for me."

Aggressively pushing past Brooke, I slam into Trey's shoulder, causing him to fall off balance. I run down the steps of our two-story townhouse and hear him mumble something to Brooke, but don't stop to listen.

I'm not even to the bottom step when the tears begin to soak my cheeks. They're not tears of sadness heartbreak over a man, they're tears of pure embarrassment. These last two days have been too much, each event trying to top the other. I can't take any more surprises.

I brush the tears away angrily.

Just as I'm reaching for the door handle of my car, Trey's hand lands on top of it, closing the door.

"What?" I snap.

"Emma, please let me explain." I look up at him and see the hurt behind his eyes. "Last night..."

I hold a hand up. I catch my sister watching us from the top step. Looking back at Trey, I keep my voice low. "I won't say anything. Just go, please."

His hand comes up to caress my face, but stops a mere inch away. His fingers twitch in hesitation. I see the tug of war in his eyes. His hand drops to his side. He lets out a small sigh in frustration.

I step back, needing to put space between us. Even though I just found out he's my coach, I'm still completely attracted to him. The magnetic pull is still present and if I don't put the distance there, I'm not sure what will happen.

"I didn't know who you were. And then—when the mask was off and I saw your eyes. The view of your entire face. Jesus, Emma," he hisses, rubbing the back of his neck. His eyes plead with mine for understanding. "I was surprised. I wasn't expecting—well, you!" He raises his hands in defeat.

"How did you know who I was? You haven't even met the team yet." I glare up at him.

He runs his hand down his face. "The roster. I have every team member's picture, stats, swim tapes and transcripts. How come you didn't tell me you were a college student when we were talking?"

I scoff. "So this is *my* fault?"

"No! That's not what I meant."

"Trey?" Brooke calls. "Everything okay?"

He looks back and holds up his pointer finger. "Just a minute."

"You better go. She's already curious. You don't want her to raise suspicion, and I have to get to practice. See you around, *Coach*."

"Emma, please. We need to talk about this." He reaches for my arm. "I knew I would eventually run into you, but—fuck," he stumbles upon his words. "I wasn't prepared for this. I thought I'd have more time to figure this all out. Let me at least give you a ride to practice so we can talk about this."

Right. That's why he came running back to my sister, because he was so concerned about me. Frustrated, I look away and down the street. It's about a twenty-minute walk from my place to the campus, so I know I'll be late, but at this point I don't care. I welcome the extra time to clear my head.

I don't look back as I turn and walk away from Trey Evans.

My sister's ex.

My swim coach.

The white-speckled tile is cold beneath my toes as I enter the aquatic center from the women's locker room. I inhale, letting the aroma of chlorine swim into my lungs. It's my favorite scent in the whole world. The smell alone can put me in a happy place. The second I step foot in here, everything else in my life disappears. The pool is where nothing can stand in my way.

The girls are spread out in the Olympic-sized pool. Some are sitting on the edge with timers, timing two girls doing a backstroke race, while others huddle in a small group working on stretching exercises. Assistant Coach Johnson is kneeling beside the pool talking to Erin, one of the girls I do the 4x100 medley relay race with. Erin looks up and notices me, giving me an enthusiastic wave.

I grin in return and walk toward the edge of the pool. Making sure my loose strands are tucked securely under my tight yellow swim cap, I maneuver my goggles down over my eyes in preparation to dive in.

"You're late," Coach Johnson barks from across the pool, causing me to halt.

"She's with me." I know that voice. Deep, throaty, and sexy as fuck.

I turn around and scowl at Trey. I know he can't see my eyes under my goggles, but I do it anyways. "No, I'm not." I shake my head, annoyed.

Coach Johnson stands up in surprise and begins to walk toward us.

Trey takes a few long strides toward me. He looks different from when I left him. Any shock, sadness, or hurt that I might have seen at my house is gone. Walking toward me is a man of confidence and authority. The man I met last night.

"Trust me, you'll want to be with me." His

voice is low enough that only I can hear.

I'm not sure if there's a double meaning behind his choice of words, but I toss them aside.

I take as much of a step back as I can without falling into the pool. "No, I won't."

"Fine." Trey steps around me and walks toward the center of the aquatic center. "Emma Peters, you're late. Swim laps until I say stop." His voice is loud and it gets the attention of the entire swim team, even Coach Johnson who stops in his tracks.

A few girls gasp, looking at one another. There are some confused faces as the girls try to figure out who Trey is.

"Excuse me?" I push my goggles up and raise my brows in surprise. I storm over to him so we're nose to nose, rage rushing through my body. "You made me late."

His lips curl upward like flames. "I offered to drive you. And I said you'd want to be with me. The choice was yours."

"You're not even supposed to be starting until Monday, so technically I don't have to listen to you."

"Coach," Coach Johnson says, taking Trey's strong hand into his. The two exchange some words.

I shake my head and then stomp off like a six-year-old child having a temper tantrum. Screw this. I'm not swimming those laps, and I sure as hell am not listening to him right now.

"I'm Trey Evans, your new head swim coach," Trey announces to the team—all eyes captivated on him, which pisses me off even more because I hate that he has the same effect on me. "I've had the pleasure of meeting with Coach Johnson and Coach Stephens to watch tapes of you ladies. I'm honored to be here and to be surrounded by such talent. With the happy news on the arrival of Coach Stephens's baby, I'll be taking over as head coach effective immediately."

I don't wait for the shocking gasps and silent cheers from the team at his announcement. I pull hard on the woman's locker-room door and let it slam closed behind me. I'm skipping todays practice. I'll come back later when I have the entire place to myself. There is only so much I can take in one day. I'll deal with the repercussions later.

I don't bother changing out of my swimsuit. I aggressively tug my jeans over and slip my T-shirt on. Just as I'm putting my shoes on, the locker-room door opens and closes. I know it's him. I can feel his presence.

"I'm not in the mood," I say in a coarse tone.

"Get in the mood," Trey hisses with venom.

I whirl around and point a finger at him. "Why are *you* mad? I get the right to be mad!" I stop myself from adding any more. Moving quick on my toes around the locker room, I check to make sure we're alone. When I don't see anyone I move to stand before him. Tipping my head up, I shoot daggers his way and tap his chest with my finger. "*You* left me naked in your bed last night, on my birthday may I remind you, and then you show up at my house today where I find out you're my sister's boyfriend, *and* my swim coach! You don't get to be mad right now."

I clench my fingers, lowering them to my side. My eyes harden. My chest rises and falls. It takes a lot to make me mad. My friends and family would describe me as the peace keeper. I hate confrontation.

Trey's body goes tense with shock. My breathing is shallow as I wait for his response, but it doesn't come. He sits down on the bench in front of me and runs his hands through his hair.

"You're right, except not about your sister. I'm not her boyfriend." His eyes lift to meet mine, and I groan in frustration. "Okay, wait." He reaches out and grips my wrist. "I panicked, Emma. What was I supposed to do? I was having the best night with you, and then it all came crashing down when I realized you were a college student. A part of my swim team. I choked. I thought you were someone else when we started talking."

"Jeez, thanks." I slump down next to him. I don't know why. I'm annoyed and should be keeping my distance.

His head slumps forward. "No, that's not what

I mean."

I peek over at him. "What did you mean then, Trey?"

"I didn't think you were twenty, okay? I thought you were older. You seemed older."

"Sorry to disappoint. If you'll excuse me, I have to go."

I begin to move, but his words stop me.

"Will you just stop being so stubborn for a minute and listen! That's the thing—I don't want you to go. I haven't been able to stop thinking about you since last night, even when I know it's wrong and I can't have you. I only agreed to meet your sister today to keep the peace between us, since she works in the administration department at the university. The last thing I wanted was for her to make a scene on Monday in front of the faculty." He stops, taking a few short breaths. "I thought about tell her about last night, but I knew I couldn't. Nothing good would come from her finding out—for either of us. When she asked me to come over, I didn't know you lived there, too. She only ever mentioned a girl named Ali as her roommate. I was left stunned, yet again."

He turns his body into me and cups my cheeks with his warm hands, his eyes darkened with pain. "I can still taste you on my tongue, Emma. When I touch you, I swear I can still feel your body writhing against me. And when I watch you talk, it's as if you've bewitched me, and when you spoke about swimming last night, my heart literally stopped for a beat."

"But?" I choke. Not that I was expecting this to go anywhere, but I thought, deep down, there was hope.

He drops his hands. "I can't have you. What happened between us never would have if I'd known who you were."

Ouch. That stings down to the nerves.

As much as his words cut me, I know they're the truth, because I would have said the same. If I'd known he was my coach, let alone the guy my sister was just seeing, I never would have pursued him.

My throat goes dry and feels rough like the

Sahara desert. In need of my own oasis, I'm unable to say anything, so I nod.

"You're an amazing woman, Emma. I've seen your tapes and have had many conversations with Coach Stephens and the dean of athletics about you. The university specifically sought me out with you in mind. They wanted someone who would continue to push you to your full aptitude. You have the potential to go far, Emma. The university sees it, Coach Johnson and Stephens see it, and I see it. You're so talented in the water, and your times are unlike anything I've ever seen. You have a real shot at the Olympic tryouts. I don't want to jeopardize your future with some scandal that would potentially hurt your future."

I lick my dry lips. "And I don't want to endanger your job, which is why I won't mention what happened between us last night to anyone."

He reaches over and rests his hand on top of mine. His intoxicating eyes glow. I feel delirious when I look into them. "As much as I want this to be something, and Lord knows I want it to be something..."

"It can't."

He drops his eyes to the floor. "It's wrong."

There's no denying the chemistry we both felt last night, and the physical attraction we have for one another is undeniable, but I know just as well as the next person that what happened was a mistake.

I stand up, grabbing my bag. Just before I leave the locker room, I turn back. Trey's elbows are pressed deep into his knees, with his spine arched forward.

With my hand on the door handle, I say, "Why is it that something that feels so right is wrong?"

I don't wait for him to answer. When his eyes snap to mine, I exit the room, leaving him to sit alone.

I know this won't be the last of Trey Evans.

Chapter Six

Our red and white townhouse is on a quiet block, just on the other side of town. It's close enough to the beach, but far enough from civilization to feel like you're away from the rest of the world.

When I push open the front door Brooke immediately stands from the couch and rushes toward me.

"Is everything okay?" There's so much concern in her voice. "I'm so sorry, Em. I wanted to tell you for this specific reason."

I arch a brow. "You wanted to tell me about dating the new head coach only in anticipation things might not work out?"

"Yes – no." She shakes her head, flustered. "I needed to know where things were going with him before I told you. It needed to be the right time."

In life, nothing is ever the right time. Things come and go when they want. It doesn't matter what stage you're at or if you asked for it. Time either works with you, or against you. In my case with Trey, it's working against me.

I'm too tired to have this conversation. I want to be done thinking and talking about Trey. "Honestly, Brooke. It's fine."

She reaches for my arm. "It's not fine if you're home early from practice. Trey said he went after you when you pushed past us to try and introduce himself privately. He wanted to take the pressure off me and make you feel more comfortable. After you walked away, he came in and said you were in shock." *That's an understatement.*

"I was, but that's not why I left practice." I lie. "I left because I'm not feeling well. It was probably all the alcohol from the party. You know I don't drink much."

She gives a small nod of understanding. "Are

92

you sure you're not mad?"

I give her a reassuring smile and slip off my shoes. "I could never be mad at you, Brooke. You're welcome to date whomever you'd like." I mean that. I'll always support her, even if that means her and Trey end up working out in the future.

Setting my bag down, I shift around her and walk into the kitchen. I grab another cookie and glass of water.

She keeps talking. "Well, I just want you to know there won't be any awkward moments on campus if we run into each other."

"Good." I take a sip.

Brooke comes to stand next to me. "I was kind of hoping he had reconsidered us breaking up." She pauses, watching for my reaction. Inside I cringe, but I keep my composure. "He said he agreed to meet me here because he wanted to make sure I was okay. He apologized for how things went down last night and definitely wants to still hang out as friends. Then he scurried off to practice because he wanted to make sure you were okay. Trey really is a gentleman."

We both got friend-zoned by the same man. I laugh inside. I have to find some humor in this messed up situation.

"He seems like a good man," I confirm. *Perfect, really.*

Brooke's eyes begin to mist over. "Sorry, I don't mean to get emotional, but why do I always fall for the perfect guy, yet he always ends up the wrong one for me?"

You and me both. "Brooke," I say her name lovingly. Wrapping my arms around her, I bring her in for a hug, doing what any great little sister would do—who had just hooked up with the man her sister liked and is referencing to. "It will all work out in the end." As the words leave my mouth, I'm not sure if I'm comforting her or myself.

Arriving at Bentwood University on Tuesday, I'm thankful for choosing a large campus. It makes it more difficult to run into the people you're trying to avoid. Moving through the packed halls, I push through the cloud of bodies that are coming from the opposite direction. A combination of cologne and coffee mixed with lemon from the recently mopped floors fills my nose.

Just as I'm rounding the last corner and can see my final destination a few steps ahead, my body comes to a halting stop as I smack into a hard object. My eyes close at the sudden impact, followed by a small groan of pain.

Hands grab each of my elbows to keep me from falling backwards onto my ass.

"What's the rush?" The voice speaks with such depth and authority.

The smell of leather takes over and it's then I realize I ran into Trey's built chest. Panic settles deep in my own chest as my eyes rake over his entire body. He's wearing black dress slacks with a nice red button-down and tie. He looks much

AMANDA MAXLYN

older, or rather more his age, than the previous times I've seen him. Small laugh lines outline his eyes, and there's a light shadow along his jaw from not shaving for a couple days. A deep crease sets in between his eyes as he drinks in my face.

"Emma?" he says as discovery awakens him.

I take back any thoughts I ever had about being thankful for a large campus. I stare up at him. *Be cool, Emma, be cool.*

A small group of girls walk by, smiling and blushing as they take in the sight of Trey. "Hi, Coach Evans," one of the girls says seductively.

I roll my eyes. Word sure moves quickly around here about the hot new swim coach.

"Ladies." Trey gives a polite head nod with a smile and wave.

"They don't even follow the swim team," I say with disgust as I stare them down like a jealous girlfriend. *Shit! Did I just say that out loud?*

When he looks back at me, I blush. It's honestly not hard for him to make anyone blush.

His jaw clicks and, my God, it's sexy as fuck.

Snap out of it, Emma! I stop fantasizing about his jaw. "I'm late," I rush. I'm not late, but it's the first thing that came to mind and, quite frankly, it sounds like a good excuse right about now. He looks devilishly handsome and I'm not sure I can handle just talking with him.

"Will I see you tonight?"

I'm momentarily speechless. He gives me an infectious grin, sending my pulse spinning.

"Huh?" I stammer.

"Tonight?" He steps closer. It's unclear if there are other students or faculty around us. I'm transfixed on Trey.

"I'm not sure what you mean." I take a step back. I can't breathe or think straight.

Space. I need space.

"Swim practice, tonight," he says.

My eyes go wide. "Yes! Of course, Trey— Coach. I'll be there." *Way to be cool, Emma. That was real smooth.*

I turn around and let out a breath of air. I begin to walk, slowly picking up the pace, putting more distance between us. Just as I'm about to round the corner, he calls out after me: "On time?"

He's teasing me, and my lip trembles with the urge to smile.

Looking back over my shoulder, I bite my bottom lip.

He lets out a throaty laugh. His eyes bore through mine, giving me a subtle look of amusement. Neither of us needs to say anything. Our unspoken words say it all. He finally looks away, shaking his head. A boyish grin present. When he turns in the opposite direction, my mouth slowly spreads wider as I watch him briskly walk away.

I'm so screwed.

"Faster!" Trey's words bounce off the walls. My arms stretch outward in front of me. My legs are bent at the knee, and my heart pounds with adrenaline as my body gives a small bounce in anticipation. My eyes zone in on Erin through my goggles. She's pushing through her butterfly stroke as hard as she can. I can see her cheeks exhale with each deep breath. Just as she touches the wall beneath me, I dive into the water, over her body. My legs kick with such strong force and my hands come together at a point above my head. I move my body with ease underwater. When I come up for air, I push myself as quick as I can into the front-crawl stroke, kicking and pulling my arms through the thick water. With each stroke and breath my mind takes over total control of my body. I move with ease, my body doing what it loves and knows. Coming to the edge of the pool, I dive under, do a front flip, and push myself even faster through the water and up to the surface. I'm always trying to improve my time, only ever trying to impress myself, but as I push myself through the water, all I can think about is Trey and wanting to impress him. I swim faster, causing my arms to ache with each stroke and my legs to burn with each kick. My temples throb with each heartbeat. As soon as I hit the wall, I clasp the edge with my fingers and pant for air. I see my teammates doing little jumps of joy and screaming cheers around Coach Evans.

He gives me a huge grin. "Well done, Peters."

I can't wipe the grin from my face. He offers me his hand and assists me out of the water. His eyes glide over my wet body. I see the lust behind them.

Erin breaks between us, causing Trey to advert his attention. She ushers me into a brief hug. "Holy shit, Em! That was amazing to watch. I've never seen you swim with such grace before."

I try to catch my breath. "What was my time?"

Resting my hands on my hips, I look down at the stopwatch in his right hand. *52.31.* Damn.

"You beat your last time by 0.06. If you keep these times up, you'll be having every paper calling. That, I'm certain of," Coach Johnson gushes with pride as he comes to stand next to us.

My eyes look for Trey who seemed to have walked away.

Immediately, there's a hand coming from behind me, a towel in tow. *Speak of the devil.*

My fingers wrap around the soft fabric.

"That was pretty spectacular, Emma. I'm impressed."

I pat my shoulders dry, eyes locking with his as I turn around. "You are?"

His eyes are lethal. "Absolutely. That was pretty great to watch."

My heart jumps.

Water drips from my forehead, down my nose, and to my lips. A tiny flutter moves through my stomach as I watch his eyes follow the droplets.

I'm spellbound around him.

He clears his throat and breaks the eye contact. He turns to face the team. "You *all* did amazing. I'd love for you four"—he motions to me, Erin, Becky, and Kim—"to rest your muscles for fifteen and then do that race again." I swear he could have just told the girls to stand on their heads and they would without hesitation. I can almost see the drool on their faces.

"Come on girls," I announce, jumping back in the water to focus and keep my muscles from tensing up.

"As for the rest of you," Trey says to the remaining eight girls, "I'd like you to work on your individual strokes and breathing exercises with Coach Johnson. I noticed a couple of you struggling out there."

During the rest of the practice Trey helps the four of us, but I can't help but notice the extra attention he gives me. Every now and again I catch Trey's eyes on me and try to act like it doesn't affect me when really his gaze gives me intense pleasure. At one point I'm certain he's about to jump into the water and join me by the way his enthralled eyes seem to undress me when I come up for air.

When practice comes to a close, the girls parade to the locker room. Some are off to lift weights, others off to get some carbohydrates.

"Are you coming, Emma?" Erin asks, looking over her shoulder.

"Not right now. I'm going to sit in the hot tub a bit to loosen up. I'll see you later." I give her a well-mannered wave and a smile.

Turning the jets on, I get comfortable on the bench. My neck rests back against the edge and my eyes drift closed. This is my favorite thing to do after practice. Reflect, relax, and regroup—the three Rs.

"It's getting late, don't you want to go get some food?"

My eyes open to see Trey standing above me.

"I'm not hungry." *For food.*

"You just burned close to one thousand calories." His lips are in a firm, straight line.

"Do you always eat after you burn calories?" I counter.

There's a dark glow in his eyes. He doesn't answer me. I watch as he grabs a plastic chair and drags it over to rest next to the edge of the hot tub. I sit up and get into a more comfortable position, looking for Coach Johnson—who is nowhere in sight. We're alone.

"He went to the weight room." I hate that he always seems to know what I'm thinking. He did this a couple times the night we met, the other day at the aquatic center and again now. "Do you always swim like that?" he asks, with a slight rasp of excitement.

I turn casually to face him, resting my arms flat over the edge. My chin nestles on top of my left wrist.

"You tell me, you've seen the tapes."

He tilts his head to the side and gives me a look that says "Don't be coy with me."

I sigh. "I like to think I do, but no, not every practice. Tonight was just a good night."

"And why is that?"

Because of you. It's what I want to say, but don't. "Lucky, I guess." My thoughts drift back to just a few days ago when I first met Trey. Was that luck, too? Or a curse?

His hands clasp together in his lap. I watch his deep-in-thought face, looking for some clue as to what's going on inside his head. He catches me staring and my cheeks burn a crimson red.

He leans forward, curiosity creeping into his face. "What made you get into swimming?"

I'm taken back by his question. I've never been asked that before. I get out of the tub, grabbing my towel, and ponder his question. Trey gets up and grabs another chair, pulling it next to his.

I take a seat. "There's a quote by Adrian Michael—'She is water, powerful enough to drown you. Soft enough to cleanse you. Deep enough to save you.' It's hard to find something that powerful that brings you joy and to find a balance for it in your life. Since I was a young child I loved being in the water, but it wasn't until I was about ten that it evoked something inside of me. I didn't want to just be in the water or compete because I was a good swimmer. I wanted to be one with something that pleased *me*, not because it made those around me happy."

He sucks in a breath of air. His face filled with

pure admiration. "That's the best answer you could have given me." I just gave him a piece of me no one else has.

He continues to watch me tenderly. As cliché as it may sound, I swear he melts my insides. I've never felt this kind of exhilarating high before. It's different than being in the water. This is the high that flutters in the pit of your stomach when you're discovering something new for the first time and don't want to be without it. Trey can make me mad, yet I lust for him. He makes me laugh and yearn for his touch. He's capable of bringing out my deepest thoughts and want to crumble in his arms.

It's euphoric.

"What about you?"

"Me?" He points to himself with a light chuckle.

"Yes, you." My voice is playful.

"My parents put me in swim classes when I was five. My sisters swam, and were actually very talented, so I thought I'd give it a shot. In high school, I found a coach that really believed in me. He pushed me to be my best. I never became worse under his belt, but I didn't become better either. I appreciated the art of the sport thanks to him, but the summer before my senior year I joined a competitive swim team and that's when I *really* fell in love with the sport. For the first time in my life I felt whole. That team pushed me to new heights. I didn't know my full potential until that summer. Swimming became something I strived to be better at."

"Why did you stop?" I get the urge to touch him so I reach for his hand, but quickly withdraw when the gesture registers with my brain.

He takes notice –looking over at me— amusement written all over his face. "What makes you think I stopped?"

"I just assumed because you coach that you don't swim anymore," I say. "Sorry." My face falls slightly.

Trey's eyes shift above my head then back to me. His finger gently pushing my chin upward to look him in the eye. It lingers for a few beats. I'm almost certain he's about to kiss me, but then his hand falls back into his lap. "Don't be sorry. I swim, just not on the same level I used to. I dislocated my shoulder a few times doing the backstroke, which resulted in two surgeries. In college I taught lessons, and after I graduated, I started coaching high school. Eventually I got an assistant coach position at a university back home and started to coach at this level. I did some one-on-one coaching as well. I met Coach Stephens at a conference a few years back. We stayed in touch, and when there was an opportunity for me to transfer here, I took it."

I lick my lips. "I'm glad you did."

Trey leans over his chair armrest. He's so close I can feel his breath on the tip of my nose. "Me too, Emma. Me too." His finger lightly brushes against my pinky.

My lips part ever so slightly. I swear his eyes undress me as he lingers over my face and body. I have to fight my own battle, restraining myself from leaning inward to brush his lips with mine.

He blinks a few times and then looks away. "Tell me, what do you want to do after you graduate?"

"Oh, the possibilities," I joke.

He leans back, getting comfortable. "I'm serious. Have you thought about trying out for the Olympics?"

I laugh. "Of course. Who hasn't? But I think my primetime is up. Besides, I should be focusing on how I'll be paying for rent now that I'm jobless. I can't afford to think about the Olympics."

"Your time is not up. The oldest female Olympic swimmer was thirty-three. I've seen your tapes and, after watching you in person, you're really something else, Emma. I haven't seen anything quite like you. It's time you realize how great you are."

My cheeks burn. His eyes fill with lust.

I let out a heavy sigh. "My family wants me to get a business degree." I've thought about the Olympics since I was a little girl. It's been a dream of mine. Even with the support of my family, they still always try to steer me toward a more realistic future.

"But?"

"I want to swim. They say there's no future in swimming. No career. I need to make something of myself, like Brooke. Having a degree in business will give me endless possibilities according to them."

"Don't ever compare yourself to your sister. Swimming defines you. If you want to make that your career, do it." His eyes brighten.

I suck my bottom lip into my mouth. His eyes follow.

"I better get going," he says, blinks a few times, then sharply stands.

I'm too stunned to say anything, or to try and stop him. Once the door clicks shut, I'm left with the low humming sound of the fan and an unexpected void.

Chapter Seven

Friday morning—after I've already had a two hour swim practice—I'm sipping coffee prior to heading out for class. I flip through one of Ali's magazines. She's already left for work, and Brooke's making some weird breakfast omelet that's supposed to be healthy for you, but it looks more like some rotten green sponge that fell out of a garbage truck.

"Are you sure you don't want one?" she asks, arching a brow.

"Um, yeah. I'm positive." I shudder.

She laughs. "Em, it looks worse than it tastes."

There's a green leaf sticking out the side. "I'll stick with normal eggs, thanks."

"These are normal," she says. "I just added some kale and spinach."

"I'll stick with eggs that are only white and yellow in color, thanks." I take a sip of my black coffee with a pinch of sugar in it. Not too sweet, but not too rich.

She shakes her head at me, moving about the kitchen. "Want to ride with me this morning?"

There are times its nice having a sister who works where I go to college, but then there are times it sucks. For instance, riding together is beneficial, but when she reports play-by-play updates to my parents about my whereabouts on campus, my latest grade, or who I'm involved with, that's *not* beneficial.

"I only have one class this morning," I mumble with my lips pressed against my mug. "Then I'm going job hunting."

She saunters back over to me and places both hands on the counter. "You can take my car back. I'll get a ride home."

My eyes widen with interest and my heartbeat begins to pick up. "From who?"

"Oh," she waves, turning back to the stove to flip her omelet. "There's a big group of us going out for drinks and dinner."

I flip to another page. "Who's all going?" I try to pass my question off as normal conversation, but really I'm pressing to know if Trey's going. I've overheard her talking to Ali about him a couple times this week.

"Just a bunch of people."

Awesome. Can I get a more vague answer than that?

"I'll just drive myself. I don't know how long job hunting will take."

"Suit yourself." She grabs her plate with the green sponge and a glass of orange juice and heads into her bedroom to finish getting ready.

We have two practices Monday through Friday: one in the early hours of the morning and another after all classes in the evening. Today's evening practice is at three o'clock being there are no afternoon classes, so it's quite possible Trey is one of the "bunch of people" Brooke mentioned. After all, he did tell her he still wanted to hang out as friends.

I toss the magazine aside. Suddenly I'm

annoyed.

Come ten o'clock in the morning I'm outside lecture hall B. Little purple and pink flowers line the pathway that leads to the double doors. The bright orange sun beats down from the clear sky above, no ounce of wind in the air. Students are dispersed throughout the courtyard either walking to their next class, sitting around palm trees in small study groups, reading on benches, or standing amongst one another chatting and laughing.

I still have twenty minutes before my economics class and contemplate getting a little ray of sunshine, or going inside to the library.

"Hey, Em!" Erin shouts from one of the picnic tables a few yards away. "Come join us." She waves me over to the small group she's sitting with.

"Hey there!" I give her the same cheerful tone.

Paul scoots over to make room for me. "Hey, Emma," Paul sings boisterously.

"Hi, Paul."

Paul and I met last year at a swim meet. He was there with a bunch of the student body and at one of the after-parties we got to talking. He was suddenly a fan. We've never dated or even hooked up, but not for a lack of his trying. He's a sweet guy, but just not my type. He'd be better off with a woman who's capable of making him a priority, like my sister. I grin at the thought and give an inner laugh. If only she were into younger men.

I settle in next to him, silently wishing it was Erin who scooted over.

He leans in. "Are you pumped for your race on Monday?"

I'm racing in the individual 100-meter freestyle and 4x100 medley relay. My eyes light up at just the thought of Monday's race.

Just as I'm about to answer, I spot Trey being

swarmed by a few eager twenty-somethings who are hoping to get more than just a light conversation with the swim coach. His sharp and assessing eyes are on Paul and me. *What is he doing here?*

Trey's brows relax and his mouth breaks out into a grin when our eyes meet.

Seeing him relaxed, his hair styled perfectly and wearing comfortable jeans with a polo shirt, makes him delectable. I try to smile, but it doesn't quite happen. His eyes gravitate over me, which makes it harder to move mine away. He's enthralling.

"Earth to Emma?"

Turning to Paul, I see he's waiting for a response.

"I'm sorry, what?"

"Are you getting pumped for your race on Monday?"

I shake my head to break up the images and thoughts of Trey. "Sorry—I am! I think we're all pumped. We've been practicing really hard."

"Against Georgia, correct?"

"Uh-huh." I can't focus knowing Trey is just a few feet from me.

My eyes flick back to him. He's still watching us. Or rather *me*. I give him a look that says, "What?" He licks his lips and then focuses his attention on the girl who's been talking to him this entire time.

I roll my eyes. He's taunting me. He knows what kind of effect he has over me, and he's using it to his advantage.

Paul starts to ask another question when suddenly Trey interrupts him, startling me. "Excuse me, you two, but I'm going to have to borrow Ms. Peters for a minute."

"Excuse me?" I say, aghast.

"Hi Coach," Erin greets.

"Mornin', Erin." He gives her a small wave with a polite smile.

"Now," he says back to me. His body tense.

"I'm hanging out with Erin before class," I shoot back.

"It's important," he insists.

"Go on, Emma. I'll meet you in class," Erin

urges.

"See, she'll meet you inside." Trey's eyes are dancing with humor. *He finds this funny!*

He bends down to pick up my bookbag by my feet. Before he stands, his hand briefly touches my ankle, spreading goose bumps over my entire body. With the simplest of touches I swear I can feel the turbulence of emotion coiled inside his body.

When he stands up, he hands me the bag. When I go to take it from him, his grip tightens. I'm certain, to those watching, it looks like we're having a tiny brawl, but to me, I can feel his inner struggle with my existence.

We keep our distance as we walk away from the table. Once we're away from other students I stop and face him.

I toss my hands in the air. "What was that?"

He tucks his in his pant pockets. "I don't like it."

He doesn't like it? "Excuse me?"

"You heard me." His vow is rough. His stance tall.

I turn in a small circle before stopping to rub my temples. *What is he doing to me?* We can't keep doing this.

Sighing, I look up at his unreadable face. "You're jealous of Paul?"

His jaw clenches when I say his name. "I already said that."

"No. You *said* 'I don't like it.'"

He steps closer, but still keeps a small amount of distance between us. "Fine, I'm jealous of whoever that Paul guy is. Did you date him?"

I give him a look of disgust. "What? Paul, no! We're just acquaintances."

His body relaxes. "Good."

Good? What does that even mean?

When I'm about to tell him whatever is happening between us needs to stop, Brooke walks by. Trey follows my gaze.

"You coming tonight, Coach Evans?" she asks with hope. Her pace slows, but she doesn't stop.

He smiles. "Yeah, I'll be there."

"Great." She giggles. My sister actually

giggled like she was in high school.

My heavy sigh brings Trey's attention back to me. My lips are in a firm line and my eyes draw inward as I watch my sister walk away.

Trey leans into my ear. *God, he smells amazing.* "Now who's the jealous one?"

"What?" I lean back, stunned. "No, I'm not-"

"Right." He draws out the word. His dimples out in full force.

"I'm not!" I hiss as he turns and walks away from me.

Shit. I'm totally jealous.

Chapter Eight

Diving downward through the air and into the water, I immerse myself in the cool, soft waves, becoming one with the depth of my sanctuary. With each breath I take, my body welcomes the inner power to kick my legs and pull my arms with each timely stroke. The lights underneath give off rays of light purples, whites, and blues, as I glide underneath the water. Time stands still as I silently move.

I don't push myself. I swim with ease for the pure enjoyment and stress relief of it. I get lost in my thoughts as I do what I love, which is why I don't hear when someone else enters the aquatic center. It's not until I come up for air and slide my goggles up that I see Trey standing at the edge.

I rub the shock from my eyes. "What are you doing here, Trey?"

It's after six in the morning, according to the clock hanging on the wall. I've been here alone since the aquatic center opened an hour ago.

"The pool *is* open, isn't it?" He's in swim trunks and holding a towel.

I nod, taking in his physique. It's the second time I've had the pleasure of seeing him shirtless. His muscles are carved deep, shoulders broad, defined thighs that quicken my pulse at the thought of them holding my body tight between them. He's beautifully proportioned.

"I suppose, yes."

I push back and begin a light backstroke away from him.

The sound of splashing water erupts. I try to not pay him any attention, letting him swim freely, but out of the corner of my eye I see him coming up to my left, doing the same stroke. I push faster, but he meets my pace. It's not long before we're racing to the end and diving under to come back up and head to the other end of the pool. My breathing picks up, narrowing in on my surroundings, feeling the pool and letting the water ingest me.

Coming to the end, I touch the wall a nanosecond sooner. I turn to face him. His smile is wide. He looks so young and carefree.

"Damn, that felt good," he pants, not hiding his wide grin.

"What? Losing?" My eyes playfully tease him.

"Nah," he runs his hand over his face and up through his hair. "The rush."

My smile lights my own face.

"Want to go again?" he challenges.

I soak him in. *Really* take him in. Every line on his face, the small sunspots along his shoulders, pecs that beg to be touched, and lips that yearn for mine. His dimples break through and our eyes lock.

I don't answer him. Instead, I ask, "Did you go out for drinks last night?" I try my best to pass the question off casually. This only gets me a chuckle from him.

"Yes, I did. But, before you say or ask anything else, no, I did not stay long and yes, I went home *alone*."

My eyes go wide. "Oh, I wasn't assuming you'd go home with any-"

He cuts me. "Did you?"

"Did I what? Go home with someone?"

He laughs. "No, go out?"

I shake my head. "I went job hunting."

Trey swims in a small circle around me. "How did that go?"

"Not well." I let out a laugh that echoes off the walls. "It's hard to find something that fits into my swim schedule. That's why waitressing worked out so well. The hours were flexible and the tip money was excellent."

He nods in understanding. "I'm sure something will pop up soon."

The silence grows thick between us. He watches me intently, and I'm unable to move.

Reaching forward, he brushes a wet strand of hair off my face. My eyes briefly drift closed at the softness of his fingers.

"What are we doing?" I whisper, leaning into his touch.

His body becomes alert. "What do you mean?"

"These mixed emotions. The flirty eyes, light finger touches, shoulder brushes, stares from across the room? You said it was wrong, and I know it is, but you continue to confuse me with your body language."

"Because I'm confused," he says. "I know it's wrong, but I can't stop thinking about you." His voice dances from wall to wall as it travels all around us. "You're a flame that I can't seem to blow out." His voice is much softer, as his eyes plead with mine. "It's been difficult seeing you so often, being close to you, yet unable to touch you. I want you so bad that being around you is physically painful."

I don't know why I'm doing it, but I inch closer to him. The gravity of his lips is inescapable.

"Emma," he breathes.

"What do you want, Trey?" He shakes his head, his face full of uncertainty and pain. When

125

he doesn't answer, I continue. "When you do touch me, I feel like I'm losing my mind. My body falls apart when you're near. Maybe it's just me, but..."

He cuts me off. "It's not just you. I don't know what you're doing to me, Emma. But I don't want it to stop, either."

He leans into me, our mouths hovering over one another. His warm breath sends my heart up into my chest.

My eyes dare him to kiss me.

"I surrender." It's all I need to say and all the permission he needs.

Our lips lock together—soft at first, but soon he's kissing me as if someone will walk in at any second and he'll never be able to get another taste.

His hand trails down my neck and traces the top of my breast, just above my swimsuit top.

My hands come up, eagerly sliding through his slick hair, gripping tighter. There's nothing tender about my touch. I'm rough, needing to be as close to him as I can get. He meets my pace, his hand wrapping around to my backside and squeezing. A hungry desire spirals through me. I kiss him harder, slipping my tongue into his mouth needing to taste him. He groans out in satisfaction.

"I can't stop," he pants.

"Then don't," I demand.

Trey kisses down my chin to my breast, his lips still wet and moist from our kiss. I drink in his sweetness.

I release my hands from his hair and rest them along the edge of the pool. My back rests firmly against the tile as I tilt my head back. Trey moves swiftly in front of me, shielding my body. Neither of us seems to care that anyone could walk in. We're so immersed in one another.

My body succumbs to his fingers as they explore my body.

"Trey," I beg. "Don't stop this time."

His erection presses into my center core. I wrap my legs around his firm hips, bringing him in even closer.

"I don't think I could even if I wanted to."

My blood pumps fast, pounding in my brain and traveling downward to my heart, causing it to leap and make my knees tremble with desire.

Trey's fingers trace my lips, parting them. "You know, once I take you, I won't be able to give you up, right?" I tilt my head upward slightly, swallowing. Water drips from my forehead as hairs rise at the nape of my neck. Somehow I've lost all words. "Come on." He lifts my back up off the edge. He locks my arms around his neck. Once he's certain I'm secured around him, he holds my body as he shuffles us along the pool edge, heading for the ladder. I'm certain he'll let go of me, but he doesn't. I help him with my body weight as he grips the ladder. With a small grunt, he effortlessly lifts me with him out of the pool.

"Where are we going?" I ask, searching his face.

"Somewhere more private."

I rest my head in the crook of his neck as he carries me across the aquatic center and through the men's locker room. Trey doesn't hesitate when he walks in. He heads toward the showers, and my heart quickens at the feel of his own heartbeat against his rib cage. He's equally restless.

He reaches behind my back, turning on the warm water, letting it soak us. Heat emanates from the stream.

I'm pushed up against the wall, pressed firmly against his chest with my legs still wrapped tightly at his waist. Trey doesn't waste any time before nipping, sucking, and claiming my lips, neck, and chest.

I moan when his lip coaxes my own.

His thumb trails along my inner thigh, sending a throbbing ache inside. His hips grind against mine. Steam swarms around us, shielding us in our own cocoon. I push down my swim straps, exposing my breasts.

"Fuck, you're so sexy." Trey's finger pinches my nipple before squeezing my entire breast into his palm. "I need you, Emma."

He glides my wet body down the front of his so I'm on my feet, but keeps my back against the wall. I push out of my suit, standing completely naked before him. He doesn't say another word. He uses his body to show me exactly what he's feeling.

Resting on his knees before me, water splashes atop his head. He picks up my ankle, resting my leg over his right shoulder. Scooting in closer, his hands come up and spread my lips open before him. I hear him groan with satisfaction just before he sinks in, claiming my swollen clit with his tongue. My head rolls to the side and my eyes lazily fall closed.

Trey's tongue slides in and out of me, up and down, sending small shudders of pure pleasure through my entire body. His hands cup my ass, squeezing firmly as my hips rock against his mouth.

"That's it, baby," he purrs. "Ride my face."

When I feel my insides tightening and filling up with pure bliss, I feel his left hand release from my backside. I look down with hooded eyes and watch him suck his finger, moistening it. Just as he reclaims his spot, I feel his finger gently ease inside of my ass just as his tongue reconnects with my throbbing clit.

"Trey," I cry out.

I don't want him to stop. The pleasure inside of me is unlike anything I've experienced before. It's exciting and naughty at the same time. The thrill of doing something forbidden is not only stimulating. It's provocative. Knowing what we're doing is so utterly wrong only intensifies the hunger I have for him.

Within a few beats, my body shivers and quakes at his mercy. I ride the high until he slows down, releases my leg from his shoulder and kisses his way up my stomach, breasts, neck, and, lastly, my lips.

I welcome the taste of myself on his lips. My hands claw at his back, needing to be closer.

"I don't have a condom. Are you on birth control?" he murmurs between kisses.

"Yes," I pant.

"Good because I'm going to fuck you now." He doesn't say the words looking for permission. They're direct and authoritative.

He takes hold of my arms, sliding my arms firmly above my head. The water washes over us, but it doesn't seem to faze us.

Trey uses his foot to push my legs apart. Closing in, he keeps a grip on my wrists with his left hand while his right comes down and hooks my right thigh. I wrap my leg around him and he nestles himself closer to my core, his thick erection meeting my opening. Our eyes lock as he slams himself inside of me. My body welcomes the pressure.

"Shit," he grunts between clenched teeth.

He doesn't move slow or gentle. He moves like a man that's wanted to own me for over a week now. Trey's hips thrust in and out of me fast. I meet him thrust for thrust, moaning out his name. We kiss each other devouringly. "You're so fucking tight, Emma."

I break free from his grip and rest my hands on his ass, burying my fingers into his flesh. I pull him deeper inside of me, rocking my hips against him.

I bite down onto his shoulder, tasting his flesh.

Trey hisses at the contact of my teeth, but doesn't slow down.

Swiftly, he pulls out, and twists me away from him. He pushes my body up against the shower wall so my breasts are pressed firm against the blue tile.

I widen my stance, allowing him to re-enter from behind. Looking back over my shoulder, his lips crash down onto mine the second his cock pushes back inside of me.

"Faster," I plead.

Trey obliges. He grips my hip, fingers digging in.

He frantically moves in and out of me. My forehead leans forward on the wall as he continues to take me. His lips kiss the nape of my neck, setting my skin on fire with his touch.

"You feel amazing, Emma. I can't get enough of you," he huffs between thrusts. "Once I've had you in the shower, I'm taking you in my bed."

I don't argue. This is one thing I agree with him on.

"Don't stop," I demand.

"Fuck," he hisses between his teeth.

Trey makes me want to pour out all my sins. His body lifts mine to new heights as he continues to claim me. I welcome each hard, powerful plunge.

I cry out, needing more. The pressure builds through my core and starts to quake.

"Hold on, baby," he requests.

But it's too late. My body explodes around his cock, and his own release follows. He says my name softly in my ear as he lets out his own release. Slowing his pace and eventually coming to a stop, he pulls out and turns me back to him. We stare at one another. His fingers find mine.

I lean up onto my tiptoes and give him a series of slow, shivery kisses. It's the first time either of our touches are loving. We continue to work our lips together slowly, taking our time.

I don't want whatever this is to end, but at the same time I don't know where it can go from here.

Chapter Nine

Trey came into my world and changed it around. I used to think everything needed to have structure, a plan. But after being with him, I'm realizing sometimes you have to be willing to take risks in order to not miss out on something that could be great.

"Wow, Em. Where are you going?" Ali's words fracture my thoughts.

I finish painting the last bit of shadow on my eyelids. "I'm having dinner with the girls," I fib.

She steps into the bathroom and leans her back against the counter. Approval flashes across her face. "Well, you look hot for just going out to dinner."

I smile at my appearance. I've never been one to really dress sexy, but tonight I do. When

Trey asked me to join him at the house he rents with his roommate Jill, I wanted to wear something that would make his skin crawl. My hair is curled—pulled back into a mid-crown ponytail—and my make-up is soft, yet flirtatious. I found a sangria red halter dress that falls mid-thigh and paired it with gold heels that buckle around the ankle.

"We're going dancing, too," I add.

I've never been good at lying. Honestly, I hate it. Nothing good comes from keeping secrets.

Ali beams. "You deserve a good night out, foxy lady. Call or text if you need anything. I'm staying in with your sister."

The only person who can give me what I need tonight is Trey.

The drive to Trey's is quicker than I remember when I came with Ali. When I pull up and park, I see a tall blonde woman getting into a tiny silver car who I can only assume is Jill. We make momentary eye contact. She's a beautiful woman. My thoughts are quickly stopped short when I see Trey coming out of the house. I don't hide the beaming smile on my face.

He's wearing dark washed out jeans with a blue button-down that's rolled up to the elbows. His hair appears wet, possibly from a recent shower, and face freshly shaven.

How in the world did a plain girl like me capture the attention of a man like *him*?

When I meet him at the top of the steps his arms are instantly wrapped around my waist, pulling me closer against him. His mouth collides with mine. He takes his time, exploring the feel and taste of my lips. My mind drifts to imagining the pressure of his body between my thighs.

"You're going to damage me," he sighs. "You look amazing. It's a damn shame I'm keeping you locked away looking like this. There's nothing I want more than to have you on my arm for every man to know you're mine." My heart thumps loud. I take deep, calming breaths. "Come on, I have a surprise for you." He locks our fingers together and leads the way into the house. The house appears much bigger now that it's not packed with bodies.

"Was that Jill?" I ask, following close on his heels.

He looks back over his shoulder. "Yeah, I asked she give us some privacy."

"She's beautiful."

Stopping abruptly, I smack into his back. He turns and towers over me. "*You* are beautiful, Emma." Heat covers my cheeks.

I swallow hard. "I-I just mean…"

His finger glides over my lips. "I only see you." My eyes stare into his. He doesn't say anything further and neither do I. The fire builds in his eyes, illuminating the gold. "Wait here."

Finding comfort on his couch, I wait patiently while he goes into the kitchen. He doesn't take long. Within a few short moments he's sauntering back into the cooled temperature room to join me, a plate in one hand and a piece of paper in the other.

"What's this?" I ask, scooting to the edge of the couch.

He sets the plate down on the gray stoned

coffee table. In the center of the white plate is an overly large piece of chocolate cake with a lit candle in the center. "I figured since you didn't have the best birthday we'd have a do over."

My eyes mist over. I look between Trey and the cake. "This is seriously the sweetest thing ever."

He shrugs, but doesn't hide his dimples from coming out. "Considering I played a role in that night not ending well, I thought I should make up for it. I owe it to you."

"Trey…" I stand up and plant a kiss on his lips. "Thank you."

"My pleasure. Now, make a wish."

I bend down so my lips are close to the flickering flame. *Please God, don't let this one slip away.* I blow the flame out and look up at the man who can make any ordinary moment magical.

He hands me the piece of paper in his hands.

"What's this?"

"Something for you." He watches me with intense eyes.

I read the words on the paper. My eyebrows pull together in confusion. "Swim lessons at the community center?"

He looks nervous. His thumbs slide into his back pockets and he shifts side to side on his feet. "I put a call into the manager there. I mentioned the idea of offering swim lessons and she loved it, especially when I mentioned your name. She said it would be an honor to have a prestigious swimmer offering the lessons." Tears sting my eyes. "Of course, there are some details to still work out as far as pay and schedules, but I figured I'd leave that up to you two. That is, if you want to do it."

I lunge at him, catching him by surprise. My chest crashes into his as I lock my hands behind his neck. "Thank you! I love this idea."

He gives me a quick peck. "You said you wanted to do something that you were passionate about. I can't think of anything else that suits you better than this."

Trey said I'm going to damage him. He came into my life without warning and now I'm falling fast. I don't want to hold back. I want whatever this is to last, but I need to know where he stands and what he's thinking.

Moving to sit on the couch, I tug him down with me. "What are we doing, Trey?"

His fingers rub up and down my thigh. "What do you mean?"

"*This*." I point between us, exploring his face for some kind of sign. Something to tell me what he's thinking. "What is this?"

He sighs, closing his eyes. When they reopen, his face relaxes. His thumb brushes along my lower lip. "I don't know, but I think we owe it to ourselves to find out."

He leans forward, kissing the tip of my nose, and my eyes flutter shut.

"But what..."

"No *buts*," he interjects. "It's you and me, Emma. We'll figure it out as we go."

"And what? We stay in hiding?"

"Look, Emma. I'm not capable of being away from you right now. I know what the risk means for us both, and I don't want to put you in a situation that you're not comfortable with. This"—he points between us—"is what I was originally trying to avoid. I'm your swim coach."

"I don't need the reminder."

His eyes go soft. "I signed a contract with the university. Part of it states I'm not allowed any type of intimate relationship with a team member. I'm not trying to throw it in your face, but you could lose your swimming scholarship and, trust me, the last thing I want is to fuck with your future. If we're going to see this out, no one can know about us *especially* your sister. Her working for the university could only complicate things."

I exhale. "I know. And I don't want you to lose your job."

"Come here." He swings his legs onto the couch and begins to lean back, tugging my arm gently so I'm lying on top of him. Pushing my ponytail back, he keeps one hand on each side of my face. "Don't list all the reasons we shouldn't be together. Think of all the reasons why we should."

Relief breaks through my lips. "So we're doing this then? You and me?" I need to know that, no matter what happens, we're in this together.

"We're in this together," he repeats. He kisses my forehead. "Just promise me one thing."

"What's that?"

"No more sitting next to Paul."

I laugh. Not a light, I-don't-want-to-embarrass-myself kind of laugh. No, I let out the kind of laugh that starts low in your stomach and moves up into your chest and rumbles outward.

"Is that a yes?" His own amusement crosses his face.

I nod. "As long you don't flirt with anymore female students *or* faculty."

His brows furrow in. "So you want me to stop flirting with you?"

I push on his chest, playfully. "No! You better keep flirting with me."

"Good, because I like flirting with you."

"Just—you know, maybe tone it down a little when you talk to the girls."

A sly smile forms. "And how do I talk to the

girls?"

"You know!" I flash him my own open-mouthed smile.

"No, I don't." He laughs, twisting me so I flip onto my back. He settles on top of me. "How do I talk to the girls?"

I try to keep a straight face. "You smile."

He laughs so hard I'm certain the neighbors can hear. "I smile? That's it! That's not even talking, Emma."

I laugh at the silliness. "I know, but you don't know what kind of effect your smile has on women. And when you wave..."

"Oh, no! Not *that* wave!" He throws his hands in the air, laughing harder.

"Stop!" I try to scoot away from under him, but he holds my arms, keeping me pinned beneath him. "You make the girls wet in their panties with those dimples. And your kind gestures only add fuel to the flame."

I know he's well aware of the effect he has on women.

"Do I make you wet in your panties, Ms.

Peters?" He wiggles his brows.

His smile *is* infectious. "I think you know the answer to that one, *coach*."

He leans forward, kissing the top of my head. I mold into him as he clutches me tight.

"Noted. I will no longer smile or wave to other women." His tone is playful, and I can't help but let out another giggle.

I tilt my head back to look up at him, daring him to kiss and touch me.

He accepts.

Trey is unlike anything I've ever experienced, and I'm honestly not ready for whatever this is to end. Whatever the consequences may be, right now, in this moment, it's all worth it.

Chapter Ten

The next week passes in a blur. If I'm not at practice or in class, I was at Trey's house. We order in, watch movies, talk about his family back in Michigan and stay in bed all weekend. It's my own perfect escape from reality. When it's just us two, I can forget he's my coach and I'm just a student. We can be us.

"Come on, Emma! Push it!" Trey yells. His voice rings through my ears every time I come up for a breath of air. "Harder!"

My legs tingle with numbness. I'm uncertain if I'm even kicking anymore. It feels like I'm using all my upper body strength to pull myself through the water.

Loud voices begin to chant, making it difficult to concentrate. I try to zone everyone out and focus only on my stroke counts and technique, but outside thoughts keep intruding.

Thoughts of Trey.

Thoughts of Brooke finding out.

Thoughts of *anyone* finding out.

When I touch the wall my heart sinks. I know it wasn't my best time or form. I pant, trying to catch my breath. I don't bother looking at Trey or Coach Johnson. I can't handle the disappointment that will be displayed across their faces.

"It's all right, Emma. You'll get it next time," Erin encourages.

I rip my goggles off and toss them aside. When the numbness in my legs subside and I can feel them beneath me again, I drag myself over to the pool edge and grab a towel.

"Emma, that was awful," Trey spits, his footsteps coming up behind me. "What was that in there? I'm not sure if I was watching a woman who took third in last year's NCAA championship, or a girl splashing around in front of her friends."

I whirl around. "I did my best," I hiss through

gritted teeth.

He shakes his head. With a small step, he's in my face. "No, *that* was not your best. Do it again!"

There's silence among us, not even the sound of the water splashing. Everyone, including Coach Johnson, is frozen. Trey's never yelled at me, or anyone for that matter in practice. Not like this anyways.

I look at the clock. *6:59 a.m.* Practice is over in one minute. "I'm tired," I say defenseless.

He doesn't turn back to look at me. "Do it again."

"Practice is over," I object. My shoulders slump, eyes still zoned in at the time.

That gets Trey to stop in his tracks. I suck in a breath of air, afraid to let it out. He turns ever so slowly with a brow raised in question. It's the only sound in the aquatic center. He stares me down, eyes dark. "Practice is over when I say it's over."

Pushing back tears, I stomp over to pick up my goggles. Without as much as a sideways glance in his direction, I take my mark at the pool edge and wait for instructions.

"Emma!" Brooke says excitedly as I enter the administration office after practice. "I feel like I haven't seen you lately."

She's standing next to the mailboxes, collecting her daily stack.

"I know, sorry. I've been busy with practice and studying for exams." My smile doesn't reach my eyes.

"No need to apologize. Are you okay?" she asks, concerned.

"Just a tough practice. Nothing I can't handle." I try to sound uplifting, but I'm too exhausted.

"Hopefully tonight's practice goes better," she offers.

Fuck. For a brief moment I forgot we had practice tonight, too. "Yeah, hopefully."

"So, tell me quickly, what's new?"

It's then I remember I haven't told her about the new job. I grin at the thought. "I got a job!" I cheer a little too loud. Brooke's eyes go wide with excitement or maybe that's the look of shock from how I just announced my job to the entire office. I lower my voice, "It's at the community center. I'm going to teach swim lessons to kids." I bounce on my feet.

"Em, that's awesome. When do you start?" She glances at the papers in her hands then back to me.

"I talked to the manager earlier this week on the phone. I'm going to meet with her on Saturday to make a schedule. Once that's set, she'll post it for parents to sign up."

She pulls me into a hug. "See, and you were worried you wouldn't find anything."

I don't tell her Trey set it all up for me.

I blow out a small puff of air. "Yeah, so that means I'll have to skip out on going shopping this weekend with you and mom."

Her mouth goes straight as she sinks into a

deep thought. "Maybe I'll see if Ali would like to come with instead." Her features become more animated as she speaks. "Or, maybe we could go after you meet that woman?"

"Possibly, I'm not sure what we're doing yet."

"We?" Her voice rises in suspicion. "Are you seeing someone?"

"No!" I'm quick to respond. Almost too quick. *Shit.* "I just mean the team. I don't know if we're practicing yet or not."

She watches me intently. "You rarely have Saturday practices."

I recall the one right after my birthday. "Sometimes we do."

She looks at her watch, "Okay, well just let me know. I have to get to work."

"I will." I turn around and bite my lip in frustration. I begin to walk over to the financial aid department to talk about some paperwork I received in the mail about my scholarship, and then Trey walks into the offices.

After this mornings practice I'm not sure I want to talk to him.

"Emma." He stops, stunned. A slow smile begins to form on his face, but then falls flat when Brooke's voice interrupts.

"Hi Trey, how are you?" Brooke comes over to stand next to us, brushing her fingertips on his hand.

His eyes bounce between us. *Awkward.* "Brooke, hi. I'm well. How have you been?"

"Great! Say, do you know if there's swim practice this weekend? Our mom invited Emma and I home to spend some time together, but Emma here"—she nudges my shoulder—"said she wasn't sure if there was a practice."

"I don't be..." His voice fades when he catches me scrunching my eyes together. Quickly, he changes his tune. "Actually, the more I think about it, yes."

Brooke's face falls. "Oh, that's too bad." Her hand rubs his arm and his eyes drop to watch. "Say, you should come out with some of the faculty members later this week. I'm sure you could use a break from coaching." She sounds optimistic.

"Yeah, maybe." When he flashes her his smile I can see her buckle. Watching them engage in light conversation makes me wonder what it would be like if they were together. I take in both of their facial expressions and watch their eyes as they continue to talk.

Brooke keeps grinning in awe. "Great! Well, I'll text you details."

"Perfect." He waves as she walks away.

Jealousy creeps in. As much as I don't want it to, I can't fight it off. When he looks over at me and sees my blank face, his mouth immediately turns down, and his hand falls to his side. "Shit, sorry. I did the smile-and-wave thing."

A small giggle escapes. "You're fine," I whisper, looking around. The office is moving about its normal business, with faculty on the phones and computers and students walking around and not paying us any attention. "I don't expect you to not smile or wave."

I can sense the hesitation in Trey's body posture. He shifts uncomfortably and holds his hands tight in fists at his side, fighting the urge to touch me.

"Sorry about this morning." The corners of his mouth turn down. A heavy sigh is my only response to his apology. "Emma, I only push you because I know you have it in you to do better. I care and want to see you succeed. It's what I was hired to do."

I can't look him in the face. I hate the feeling of letting him down.

Letting *me* down.

"I know. I wasn't my best this morning. This week has been crazy. My mind was too full today." My eyes meet his. He knows what I mean. It's been a whirlwind romance between the two of us.

"Come with me," he orders.

"What? I need to talk with financial aid," I protest.

He doesn't add another word to the conversation. He exits the office and I follow quickly behind him.

"Coach Evans?" I holler down the hall after him, but it only causes his pace to quicken.

We turn down the hall toward the aquatic center. The place is deserted. His office light is off and he doesn't bother turning it on when he enters. I stop and look behind me.

"Come in," he instructs. "Quickly."

When I step in, he takes hold of my hand, lacing our fingers together. "Say it again."

"What?"

"Coach Evans." The warmth of his smile matches his voice.

"*Coach Evans*," I purr.

"So sexy." He pulls me in for a tight hug. "Gosh, I missed you. It's been too long." He breathes in my scent.

"I just saw you last night *and* this morning."

"My point exactly."

"Trey," I breathe. He brings me over to his desk. "What are you doing?"

"I have thirty minutes before my meeting with Coach Johnson about the upcoming conference meet." He gently backs me up to his desk and prompts me to sit. Spreading my legs apart, he steps between them and I welcome the closeness.

"Thirty minutes?" I raise my eyebrows seductively.

"I get you for at least twenty of those." He nuzzles into my neck, brushing my hair to the side.

"Trey?" Panic sets in. "Someone could walk in."

"The lights are off." He sucks on my earlobe.

"So? There's no lock."

He hesitates, but eventually steps back. Looking around the room, his eyes light up. He scoots one of the chairs over to block the door. "There."

Because that won't raise suspicion if someone tries to get in.

Trey's fingers intertwine with mine. My body pulses with nervous energy at the thought of him burying his cock deep inside me and me crying out his name.

He looks over at me, and my skin prickles with goose bumps. His eyes are filled with intense desire.

"We don't have that much time."

"We won't need it." I press my lips against his and hook a finger in his belt loop, pulling him closer.

He groans.

His tongue parts my lips and I welcome the entrance. One hand grips my waist and another finds my thigh, slowly trailing upward. My clit throbs, begging to be touched.

He breaks our kiss. "You look so fucking hot in this dress." His eyes ravish my body, sending an electric current down my spine. His face turns more serious as he looks into my eyes. "What are you doing to me, Emma?"

Heat creeps across my cheeks and down to my chest. Trey traces my blush with the back of his hand. I reach up, touching his fingers. Picking up my palm, he kisses the inside of my wrist.

"What are *you* doing to me?" I whisper, looking back at him through lust-filled eyes. I've only known him for a short time, but I'm almost positive what I feel towards him is love.

"Come here." He tilts my chin upward and gives me the lightest of kisses. Our mouths explore one another more tenderly. The fire builds between us as our hands run up and down each other's bodies. I want to get to know every part of this man's body.

I suck on his tongue and he moans. His hands grip the soft fabric of my dress tighter and I deepen our kiss. He moves more impatiently. I love the ache he has—the ache he has for only me.

Taking his right hand, I slide it down my body so it rests between my thighs.

"You're making me so wet," I say. He hisses under his breath. "Touch me," I demand.

His left hand holds me in place as his right pushes my dress all the way up. My head rolls back as the ache between my thighs increases with the anticipation of being owned by Trey. My hands come down to clasp his desk. He moves the soft fabric of my thong down my legs, stopping just above the knee, and presses me flat against the desk. He steps back, but never takes his eyes off of me.

"Do you know how exquisite you are,

Emma?"

Hearing him say those words makes my stomach flip and my clit pulse.

His fingers hook the top of my thong and slip it the rest of the way off. A cool rush of air hits the bare skin of my folds. My body trembles, getting ready to be broken free with ecstasy.

Like a bolt of lightning, he unzips his pants and positions himself between my thighs. He cups the back of my thighs and positions my legs around his waist. His erection pushes against my slick folds, and he slides inside me with ease. My hips buck with his and we move impatiently.

"Shit," he moans. "You're always so ready for me."

"Fuck me," I moan out in erotic pleasure. Trey listens, pumping his hips faster, awakening the flames inside of me. "Yes," I cry.

A light sheen of sweat covers his face. "Take it deep, baby." Trey pounds into me. "My cock loves being inside of you."

I don't think I'd ever *not* want his cock inside of me. I roll my hips beneath him. Our bodies fitting together as one. The wood from the desk digs into my palms when I tighten my grip.

"Touch yourself," he pleads. His eyes filled with hunger. "I want to watch you rub your clit as I finish inside of you." I suck in a sharp breath of air. I've never touched myself there in front of a man before. "Don't hesitate."

I unclamp my right hand from the desk and find my swollen bud. I start rubbing in slow, gentle circles, but when Trey picks up the pace so does my fingers.

Trey moans my name. His body bursts free of his own burning sensations at the same time I crumble within.

He pulls out before I even have my eyes open. He helps me up and off the desk, giving me a long, passionate kiss.

Once we've both respectfully put ourselves back together, he turns the light on and puts the chair back in its correct spot.

He grips the door handle, but doesn't open it. "How about I come over Saturday and cook for you?"

"Like, you come over to my house?"

He chuckles. "Yes. We've only been to mine. I'd love to see where you spend your time when you're not with me."

"You've been to my house." My mind flashes back to when he came over to talk to Brooke.

"Yes," he confirms. "But, I'd like to see where you sleep." He hovers over my face. "And think of me."

"Trey..." I lick my lips.

"Come on." He opens the door and holds it for me to step out. Coach Johnson is already walking down the hall. "Just in time," Trey murmurs.

"Thanks for taking the time to stop by and discuss this mornings practice."

"And thank you for your time." I wave goodbye to Trey and nod hello to Coach Johnson as I walk steadily down the hallway. When I round the corner, my phone beeps.

Coach Evans: We'll continue this discussion later about me coming over on Saturday.

I look at the text. I quickly type back *okay*

and hit send.

Chapter Eleven

The clock ticks in the silence. My head bobs with the second hand as I watch Ali pour herself some coffee in a to-go mug.

"Are you sure you don't want us to wait for you?" Brooke grabs her purse. "We can hang out for a few hours. I could tell Mom we'll be a little later?"

My pretend practice is in an hour. "By the time I get home from practice and cleaned up, it will be too late with the drive."

"There's always tomorrow," Ali offers. "We don't have to go today." She doesn't look at us when she speaks.

It's one o'clock and I've been trying to get them out the house for the last thirty minutes since I got home from my meeting at the community center.

My stomach is filled with nerves. I don't know why I couldn't have just gone over to Trey's house. It would have simplified the situation. "Honestly, you two go and have fun. Tell Mom I said hi and I'll make the next shopping trip."

My phone beeps. I look around, but don't see it. *Shit.* "Have you seen…"

Ali picks it up, cutting me off mid-sentence. She's looking at my screen. "Here, it's Coach Evans." She hands me the phone and I yank it from her hands. I look out the corner of my eye and see Brooke go still.

"Why is he texting you?" She looks at me with curiosity.

I shrug. "Probably related to practice. You know." I pass it off as if it's normal.

"Why does Trey have your number?" she prods.

I become defensive. "He's my coach, Brooke. We have to communicate."

She sighs. "Sorry, you're right."

I look at my screen.

Coach Evans: I'm waiting...

Me: I'm trying...

He's so impatient sometimes!

I stand up from the couch and head to the door in a quick, erratic pace, hoping that will get them out faster. My paranoia is getting the best of me. I can't stop myself from sweating and *really* want to jump in the shower.

Brooke looks dejected. "Okay, well have a good day."

"Thanks." I open the door all too quickly for her.

"Are you pushing me out?" Her eyes raise with skepticism.

"No! I just need to get ready for practice and I know how Mom gets. She'll be calling you any minute asking if you're on the road yet."

Ali shakes her head in agreement. "That does sound like your mom."

"Okay, we're out of here." Brooke closes the door behind them and I immediately dive for my phone on the coffee table.

Me: They just left.

Coach Evans: It's about time! Be there soon.

Me: I need to jump in the shower. The door's open.

Coach Evans: Why? You're just going to get dirty again.

Me: I'll be quick.

Coach Evans: Not when I'm there you won't be. We'll be taking our time.

I race up the stairs. Even though I just came back from the community center, I'm nowhere near ready for Trey to be here. As I grab a towel from the hallway closet, I hear the front door open. *Fuck! What is Brooke doing back?*

"Brooke?" I yell from upstairs.

"It's me," Trey answers.

I shriek. "Trey?"

"Are you expecting someone else?"

I laugh. "No."

"Good." Footsteps come upstairs. I head into my bedroom to grab an elastic band from atop my dresser and toss my hair up in a messy bun. "Which door is yours?"

"Third from the left." My hands work fast, trying to find a home for the loose hairs. I rub my face to try and add some color, and I wipe my eyes, hoping they don't appear tired.

Trey pushes my door open and takes two steps so he's in front of me. His face is freshly shaven, hair styled, and he's wearing jeans with a green and white sweatshirt. He flashes me the dimples I love so much and my body floods with warmth.

I brush my lips to his. "How did you get here so fast?"

He inhales my scent. "I was outside, down the road, waiting."

"Stalker much?" I tease.

He gives me a sardonic smile the same time he trails his fingers up and down my sides. "You said they'd be gone by 12:30, so I headed over around that time, but Brooke's car was still in the driveway. I went around the block and waited for the secret signal." He winks.

I let out a snort. "Secret signal?"

"Double-Oh-Seven style, baby."

I shake my head at his silliness.

Trey takes notice of the towel next to me. "Can I watch?" He wiggles his brows.

"No!" I swat his chest playfully and scoot out of his arms. "I'm all gross."

He grabs my arms and swings me around in a circle. My head falls back in laughter. "You're never gross. Don't say that."

I look down at my appearance. "Look at me!"

"I did, and I like." His eyes light up like a flame and I blush. He kisses the tip of my nose and I melt in his arms.

"I stopped at the store and got food to cook up some lunch. I also picked up a movie for us." I stand still, soaking him in. I'm amazed that this man, who is twelve years my senior, wants to cook for me and lounge around watching movies.

"*Sweet Home Alabama?*" I draw out the words with a hint a laughter. I love that he's a romantic at heart.

He chuckles. "That *is* a good one, but no."

I think of other ways we could occupy our time. "I didn't think you'd want to watch a movie."

"What? You thought we'd be having sex all afternoon?" When I don't say anything he holds me back at an arm's length. "You're a naughty girl, Emma Peters."

I roll my eyes.

"Come on, let me cook for you." He takes hold of my hand and leads the way down the stairs.

"I haven't showered!"

He stops and winks. "Good thinking. We can skip the main course and go right for dessert."

"*Trey*," I warn with a sideways glance.

"You laugh now, but later you'll be screaming my name."

I gulp. My thighs clench together at the thought. Sex with Trey is exhilarating. The way our bodies join together is explosive and nourishing all at the same time.

"If there's enough time," I taunt.

"Oh, there will be plenty of time." He makes

himself comfortable behind the kitchen counter and begins emptying the brown paper bags. "I hope you like stir-fry."

"I love it. Brooke makes a really good one." I say the words not realizing I said them. When I look away, Trey comes over and takes my hand, giving it a kiss.

"Don't get like that." His lips press into my knuckles.

"Like what?"

"It's okay to talk about your family. I want to hear about them." His voice is gentle.

"It's just weird." My shoulders bounce and I look away. Talking about her with him makes me uncomfortable.

He walks back over to the counter and I move to grab him a pan, cutting board and knife. "It's only weird because you're making it. So your sister and I hung out," he says. "It's not a big deal."

"You did more than hang out, Trey. You two dated."

He spirals around and pins my back against

the pantry door. His breathing becomes shallow. "We went on a few dates, yes. I can't deny that. We also went out a lot with other faculty. We did more texting than talking on the phone. We kissed once, and I was a gentleman because I held her hand and opened the door for her on one or two occasions. What I had with her was more of a friendship than a relationship. Please don't think it's weird talking to me about her. It doesn't hurt me, or make me uncomfortable. As a matter of fact, I encourage it."

"Okay."

"Good." He gives me a tender kiss. "Better now?"

"One more question, then we can continue our date."

His lips lift at the corners. "Date?"

I roll my shoulders. "Well, considering we can't go out in public together, this is as close to a date we'll get."

He cocks an eyebrow. "Emma, I think we're past the dating stage."

Is that him calling me his girlfriend? My heart

flutters.

"Now, one more question. Then I'm going to cook for you." He wraps his hands tighter around my waist.

"Does our age difference bother you?" We've yet to have this conversation and if we're past the dating stage than I think it needs to be addressed.

"No." He's quick to reply, no hesitation. "Does it bother you?"

Does it? I think about it for a moment. I know I've questioned myself if he should be with a woman more his age, but I haven't actually been *bothered* by the difference?

"Not at all," I answer truthfully.

"Good." He begins to chop a green pepper. And just like that the topic is dropped. "How'd the meeting go this morning?"

Wow. This feels so domesticated. I settle in at the breakfast bar. "Great! She posted a sign about the swim lessons earlier in the week and has been getting interest. We set the schedule for two forty-five minute classes on Saturdays and two one hour classes on Sundays. As more interest comes in and classes fill, we may add a couple more. It just depends on where the demand is and if we can work around the conference meets. In the summer I'll do Monday through Friday."

"That's awesome, Emma. It sounds like it's all falling into place. When do you start?" he asks, slipping out of his sweatshirt. His white T-shirt raises slighting. My gaze wanders over his body. I want to reach and trace every inch of him with my fingertips and mouth.

His mouth spreads wide. "See something you like?"

Embarrassment flushes through me. A rush of heat fills my cheeks.

"Uh-I," I begin to stammer.

His mouth locks with mine, his tongue spreading my lips apart. His hands cup my cheeks and I whimper in surprise. When his tongue brushes tenderly against mine, I match his pace. He doesn't deepen it. The contact is brief, yet stimulating.

When he pulls back, I'm paralyzed.

"This body is all yours, Emma. Never feel ashamed for checking me out. I do it to you every day." He gives me a devious smile.

I exhale and nod. Letting my thoughts become coherent, I answer his question about the job. "I start in two weeks. It means a lot that you helped out with this. I'd probably still be searching for a job if it wasn't for you."

"Of course." He wraps his arms around my waist. "I'd do anything to help you."

My head rests against his beating heart. "After talking with her it made me realize I want to keep my major."

"Yeah?" He draws light circles on my back.

I close my eyes at the calmness he brings. "Maybe my parents were leading me in the right direction after all."

"How so?"

"I think it would be great to open my own center and teach swimming to anyone who wants to learn. Having a business management degree will only help my dreams of being in the water and sharing my love of the sport. I don't want to limit myself or regret anything. I want to embrace my passion." He kisses the top of my head and I snuggle deeper into his chest. "Who knows what the future will hold. In a year I might be trying out for Olympics, but for now, I feel like I'm finally on the right path. And who says I can't do both?"

He squeezes me tight. "Emma..." he trails off, his voice getting lost in his throat.

I break out of his embrace. "Yeah?"

His eyes sink into me. If there's such a thing about looking into one's soul, this is the look. Love is written all over his face and in his eyes. When his lips part my heart slows its pace. I wait for him to continue speaking, but he doesn't.

"Never mind." He shakes his head, smiling.

I step back. "Say it," I insist. *I feel it, too.* I want to scream it so loud. I open my mouth but nothing comes out. I've managed to elude love before Trey so why is it when I know I've found it, it's hard to tell him? It should be easy. It's only three words. Maybe it's the fear of rejection? The

9uncertainty of where this can go? Whichever the reason may be, I know we'll say it when the time is right. You can't force it.

His lips brush mine once more as his hand moves down my body and squeezes my ass. "No more talking. Kissing, more kissing." His voice is deep and throaty. It shakes through my core.

I don't want to kiss.

I want to fuck.

176

Chapter Twelve

I give him a provocative smile. "I'm going to suck you so good you'll never want to have another mouth near your cock."

"Holy fucking shit, Emma. You can't say things like that," he groans, his head falling back and eyes closing.

"Come on," I instruct, clasping my hand with his and lead the way to the living room.

Stopping in front of the couch, I motion for him to take a seat. His eyes look at the couch then me.

"Here?" His eyes light up like coals in a fire.

I suck my lower lip into my mouth and bite. He quickly obliges, sinking into the couch.

I watch as Trey shifts, tugging at his jeans

along his upper thigh. My eyes travel to the hardness that's formed.

His eyes taunt me, challenging me to go for it.

Getting on my knees in front of him, I lean into his body. My chest perks against his as my fingers trace along his thighs and up to his cock. He sucks in a sharp breath and groans.

I begin to undo his pants and he helps, pushing them down his legs. Tugging on his boxers, his erect cock springs free. I trail my tongue along the engorged veins, taunting him. His cock twitches under my control, and I love it. His head is plump and purple, calling for my mouth. I spit, using my own saliva mixed with his pre-come as a lubricant. The moment I take his shaft into my mouth, he lets out a growl, followed by a moan. I bob my head up and down, taking him deeper into my throat. Thankfully, I don't have a gag reflex. His thick head touches the back of my throat and he calls out my name along with a few pleasured moans. As I continue to suck and lick, my free hand squeezes his balls and rolls them gently. I can tell by his cries of pleasure and breathing that he's enjoying it. I kiss down his shaft, making my way to his balls. I take one into my mouth, sucking and licking, and then the other. I smile against his burning skin.

With one hand resting on his shaft, I move the other between my legs and inside my yoga pants to touch myself. I pump his cock and suck harder. The faster my head moves, the faster I rub my swollen bud. The pressure builds underneath my fingers as Trey flexes his hips quicker against my mouth.

"Holy shit, are you touching yourself?" he asks with an approving surprise.

"Mmm," I hum against him.

"Fuck!"

A rush of salty liquid pours into my mouth just as my body twitches with its own orgasm. I release the suction around his cock, leaving us both breathless.

He leans forward, his body fully awakened. I've never seen a man look sexier than right here in this moment, after sucking him dry. His brown eyes glow as he leans in to claim my mouth.

Breaking our lips apart, I begin to stand. Trey reaches up, hooking his finger with mine.

He looks like he's ready to pounce. "You're not going anywhere."

I raise an eyebrow. "No?" I wouldn't dare leave this moment. I'm powerless when it comes to him.

"No, I'm not done with you yet."

Yet. My heart skips a beat at the promise.

Pulling me down so I'm straddling him, our lips lock together, moving uncontrollably with one another. I yank my shirt over my head and toss it behind me. Trey's hand slides under my bra and lifts it up, exposing my breasts. His mouth kisses my skin. His vitality capturing me.

"I want to take my time with you, Emma, but I can't. I want your body too fucking much to move slowly."

I'd take fast and rough or slow and tender. Either way sex with Trey is like an explosive current.

We're so zoned in on one another that we don't hear the front door open.

"Em, you here? We're back!" Ali's voice cuts our panting.

Instantly, I freeze and Trey drops my nipple from his mouth.

"Oh, shit! Sorry!" I watch as Ali turns around, moving in circles, unsure where to go. She covers her face. "Don't worry! I didn't see—um—much."

"Fuck," I shout. Trey helps me off his lap and quickly pulls his boxers up.

Ali stands with her back to me, hands covering her eyes. I pull my bra back into place and look for my shirt.

"You said you wouldn't be back until after nine!" My blood rushes through my body. "It's been like … an hour!"

"Your mom wasn't feeling well, so we grabbed a quick bite instead," she rushes out in defense.

Trey stands up, and it's that moment when my sister walks in.

"Trey?" She freezes, too stunned to move, looking between us. Her eyes flash to me and then to Trey, who is zipping his pants up. "What

181

the fuck?"

Trey runs a hand through his hair, mumbling something.

"Look, Brooke," I begin, but she cuts me off.

"No, Emma, I've already seen enough. What in the hell is going on? How long have you two been fucking behind my back?"

My lips tremble. I try to speak, but Trey senses my tight throat. "Almost a month now. We met the night of Emma's birthday."

My eyes flash to Ali. I watch as recognition paints her face. She looks between Brooke and me and then between Trey and me, followed by Brooke and Trey. "Holy fucking shit," she murmurs.

Brooke's eyes darken. "So, what? You broke up with me because you wanted to fuck my sister?"

Trey shakes his head. "No, it's not like that. We met afterward. She was sad about losing her job and it was her birthday and I felt bad after our night. It just happened."

What the fuck?

"Yeah, it sounds like you felt bad. You

couldn't even wait a minute before hooking up with my sister." Brooke storms over to me. "How could you do this to me?"

I hold my hands up, apologetically. "Brooke, I didn't know!"

"Don't lie to me! You know damn well who he is." Her face fills with red.

"I mean that night! I didn't know who he was."

"He knew!" She points at Trey. "He had the swim team roster. He knew what you looked like. He also saw pictures of us on my phone."

Trey takes a cautious step toward Brooke. "She was wearing a mask. It was dark, I wasn't thinking. I *didn't* know until…"

"Until what?" she presses. "You fucked her? So that's your thing, Trey? Hooking up with young college girls?"

Trey's face falls and shoulders slump forward.

"Okay, let's all take a breather for a moment." Ali steps into the conversation. Turning, she looks at Brooke. "In Trey's defense, Emma *was* wearing a mask and it was difficult to recognize her. Even I wouldn't have known it was her."

"You're defending him now?" Hurt sinks into Brooke's eyes.

Ali looks around the room. "I'm not defending anyone. I'm simply pointing out a fact."

"Well, facts aside, he knew who she was afterward and they still continued with their charades."

"Brooke! Stop," I yell. "Trey stormed out of the room the second he found out who I was. I didn't have a clue who he was until he showed up here the next morning." My breathing picks up and I compose myself. In a much lower and calmer voice, I add, "We tried to fight it, but we couldn't. I *really, really* like him, Brooke. *A lot*. And I know he feels the same. I want to be with him, and I'm certain he wants to be with me. I'm sorry you found out this way. We didn't want to hurt you, or anyone for that matter." I take a small step toward Trey, linking my pointer finger with his. Brooke's eyes follow.

"End it," she spits with venom. "End it now or I

go to the dean."

"Brooke." Trey releases me and takes a long stride so he's in front of her. "Don't do this, please. I'm in love with her." I suck in a breath. *Holy shit. I was not expecting that right now.* "I'm sorry you found out this way, but please, I'm begging you to hear us out."

Her eyes are ice cold as she looks between us.

"Brooke?" Ali whispers. "Maybe we should go cool down for a bit."

"No," she interjects. "End it now or I go to the dean." She looks over at me, but I don't see my sister. I see a woman who is seething with anger.

"Brooke, please. Just listen," I plead.

She continues to stare Trey down. "Finish it or I swear I'll finish it for you."

"Okay," Trey ratifies.

Okay? Just like that? "What?" My head draws back and my muscles tighten. My eyes fill with tears. "Trey?" He doesn't answer me. "Trey!"

Trey glances my way, his eyes unrecognizable. "I won't mess with your future,

Emma."

I watch, dejected as he walks to the door. When I begin to move after him, he halts. "Don't," he commands. He doesn't bother putting his shoes on. He just picks them up and walks out the door without a glance back at me.

My shoulders slouch and tears fall freely. "Brooke, why are you doing this to me?"

"He's thirty-two, Emma. Do you really think it will go anywhere?" She walks past me and starts heading up the stairs to her room. "Don't tempt me, Emma. I'll have him out of that school in a heartbeat if you two even think about each other in any way that's not related to swimming."

I fall to the floor, clutching my stomach. Ali comes over, embracing me. She rubs my back and clutches me tight against her.

I cry hard as I think about this past month.

I should have said no.

I should have walked away.

I should have ended it.

But I didn't.

And now I'm left aching in the absence of his

presence.

Chapter Thirteen

I try calling and texting Trey the rest of Saturday and all day Sunday. He doesn't answer. I can't sleep. Every time I try, my mind return to its torturous play-by-play of events. Brooke refuses to talk to me or even look in my direction. On Sunday, I hear her crying to Ali, telling her how much I hurt her and how wrong my relationship with Trey is. It's funny how things come back full circle. A month ago I was listening to Brooke defend and apologize for her and Trey, and now, here I am trying to do the same.

Monday morning I head straight for his office. When I see that the lights are off, I walk to the aquatic center, not bothering to change in the locker room first. I walk through the halls feeling like a zombie, moving through the motions, but not paying attention to anything around me.

I know Trey can't afford to miss our practices with our upcoming conference meet and the ACC championship fast approaching. My eyes immediately scan for him when I enter. The men's swim team is just finishing up their practice. Jake, one of the guys on the team, notices my presence before anyone else.

"Emma, did you come to finally accept my challenge to a race?"

I give my best attempt at a smile. "Not today, Jake. I just came to watch my second favorite team while I wait for the girls to arrive."

He swims to the pool edge. "Aw, come on? We're just finishing up anyways."

The main door opens and in walks Trey with Coach Johnson and the men's assistant coach. Trey's eyes find mine almost immediately and I stand up. His shoulders relax. I ignore Jake's call for me to come back as I walk over to the coaches.

"Coach, can I talk to you for a minute?" My

eyes implore Trey's. "Please?"

Small beads of sweat line his forehead. He shoves his hands into his athletic pants. "Um, right now isn't really a good time."

I swallow the hard lump forming in the back of my throat and beg my wet, dull eyes to fade away. "Okay."

My shoulders slump.

"Trey, go ahead, man. We'll reconnect afterward," Coach Johnson offers.

Trey doesn't say anything. He just walks away. I quickly follow him down the hall and to his office. I can feel the tension between us as we walk in silence. He doesn't look back to make sure I'm following or offer to hold the door open for me. Once we're behind his closed office door, I give up on holding back the tears. My heart aches and I can't let things end like this.

"Emma, please don't cry." He hesitates, reaching up, and then drops his hands back to his sides and tucks them away.

"Why are you doing this? We can figure it out." *Great, I sound like my sister, pining after a man who has rejected her.*

He steps forward now. I can smell the leather and wood scent on his clothes. I crave to be closer. "I'm protecting *you*. I told you that I don't want you to lose your scholarship. I could care less right now about this job. I'd quit tomorrow if it meant keeping you safe on the swim team and in good standing with the school."

"Then quit," I blurt out. Immediately I regret saying those words. It's selfish to ask that of anyone, let alone the person you're in love with. "Can't we go to the dean together? You're only filling in for this season, right? Coach Stephens will be back next year."

The room goes cold at my words. I try to banish the thought, but it's then that everything comes clear. Trey won't be here next year. This was only temporary.

His eyes flick to mine. He knows it, too. "Don't think like that, Emma," he says. "We would have figured it out."

"How? We never discussed your future plans. We only talk about *my* future. You never told me what you were planning on doing after the season ended. Were you planning on staying here?" I wait for him to reply, but his absent words are the confirmation I was looking for. "You said you loved me."

"I do!" He takes my hands in his, bringing them to his lips and kissing each knuckle tenderly. "When you asked me what we were doing, I answered truthfully. 'We'll figure it out as we go.' I didn't know the answer because I knew there was the possibility I wouldn't be here come March. I hoped, but my contract only goes until March 1, with a contingency on the ACC and NCAA championships. Then I would stay to see *you* on."

"And you didn't think what would happen to us?"

"I didn't plan for us to happen *or* for us to get this deep, so I didn't let myself think that far ahead. Your sister threatening to tell the dean would hurt you more than it would hurt me, and I refuse to allow that to happen. I have a university waiting for me in Michigan that would take me with open arms regardless."

"And you know that, why?"

"My father's the dean of faculty in Michigan. He'd bury any story that followed me there."

I nod. He has someone to make his problems go away, while I have someone who only makes mine worse.

"So what now?" There's soreness in my lungs and throat. I know the answer to the question, but I need him to say it.

Still holding my hand, he gives it a small squeeze before immersing my entire body in a tight grip. "You get to keep your scholarship."

My shoulders begin to quake and my heart swells.

"Your needs and future are more important to me. There will be a time for us, Emma," he soothes.

"Just not now," I say between sniffles. "What about my need for you? That's important to me!"

"Emma, please." He brushes away the tears with the pads of his thumbs.

I step back and clutch my chest. "You don't

care about us."

His eyes close and his body shifts. "It's because I care that I'm letting you go."

I choke out a sob. My heart feels like it's twisting inside my chest, filtrating pain through my bones. Numbness clouds my eyes and despair bathes in my blood. A hollow feeling takes shelter in the pit of my stomach.

Love is selfless.

Trey is selfless.

There's a soft knock on the door. I rub my eyes and tuck my head down as I slip out. The happiness I felt a few days ago, and the hope I held onto just moments ago, is now depleted.

Chapter Fourteen

Trey misses practice on Tuesday and Wednesday. Coach Johnson tells the team he had some personal things come up and would be out the rest of the week, but assured us he'd be at the race against Boston. I tried to appear unaffected, but I was barely holding it together inside. On Thursday I say I'm sick and stay home in bed.

Friday morning I force myself out of bed. The pain is so profound. It feels like I've broken something deep inside my body, but everything appears to be intact. I can still feel my heart beating, so I know it hasn't split into two like people say a broken heart does.

I've detached myself from everything I

thought I knew over the last month with Trey. I lived in a fantasy with him and coming back to reality really fucking hurts.

When I make it to practice, I sit in the corner off to the side and begin to stretch. Erin comes walking in a short second later with a female I've never seen before. She's wearing a black pencil skirt and purple blouse with her hair pulled back in a tight bun at the nape of her neck. In one hand, she's carrying a briefcase and in the other is a stack of folders. She laughs at something Erin says. Curious, I try to listen in, but can't hear anything. I've never been good at reading lips, but I try and fail miserably. As they walk by and the mystery woman's eyes flick to mine, I quickly look away, trying not to make it obvious that I was attempting to eavesdrop. I begin to stretch, my pulse quickening. Just as I look up, I see Erin pointing over at me.

Shit.

My breathing picks up and my heart falls.

"Hi, you must be Emma," the mystery woman says as she walks over to me. Her heels snap against the tile. "I'm Rebecca. I'm with the university board of directors."

"Hello." I swallow.

"I was hoping I could borrow you for a few minutes before you begin your practice?"

"Oh, um." My eyes dart nervously around the room. "Sure."

Brooke did it. She went and told on Trey even when he did what she asked.

"Great, will you come with me to the dean of activities office?" She offers a warm smile. I try to read her face, but I can't.

"Of course." My hands begin to shake and my knees start to tremble.

I slip a pair of university sweats over my swim suit. Trying to hide my nervousness, I shove my hands into the front pocket of the sweatshirt.

They know. They have to know.

I have two options. One, run out of here and never look back. Or two, face whatever is about to be thrown my way and accept the consequences. I choose option two. I'm willing to accept my fate.

I see Brooke standing outside the dean's door just as I enter the main office. My eyes go wide. When she sees the dumbfounded look on my face, her eyes crease inward. "Emma? Don't you have practice?"

Rebecca is right behind me so I don't have much time. I fume at Brooke. "What did you do?" I don't care about the looks we get from the staff, which is in close proximity. I refuse to hide my frustration. She shakes her head, baffled. "I don't know what you're talking about."

I shake my head. "I can't believe you would do this."

Rebecca comes to stand next to me. Brooke soaks her in then looks between us. Her eyes squint in confusion.

"Ready?" Rebecca asks.

I force myself around Brooke and into the dean's office. He stands immediately when he sees Rebecca and me.

"Emma!" Brooke exclaims from behind me. I ignore her, but she follows anyways.

"Good morning." My voice shakes. I bottle

up my frustration toward Brooke and try my best to appear calm and collected, but really my insides are twisting with mixed emotions of nerves and anger.

"Thanks for coming. I wouldn't normally ask you to come here during a practice, but I missed you yesterday and I'm afraid I have a meeting shortly that I have to attend to, but I was hoping I'd be able to discuss something with you."

I look back at Brooke, who is standing in the doorway. She looks just as nervous. Her chest freezes and any color that was on her face is now gone.

"Um, of course," I falter.

"Coach Evans has been given a few days off." *Oh, shit.* I'm not sure if I gasp out loud or not, but my hands cover my mouth. I wait, with my mouth hanging open for what's to come next. He gives me a questioning look, but presses on. "He was supposed to be attending the faculty gala next Tuesday, but I've been informed he won't be attending."

"You see," Rebecca cuts in. "He was going

to be presenting Coach Johnson with the Outstanding Coach Award. I brought the idea up to the dean about having *you* present the award to Coach Johnson instead."

I look around the room. *Is that all? Is Trey not fired?* "That's what you wanted to talk to me about?"

Rebecca nods.

I'm so relieved. My posture relaxes. I hear Brooke sigh behind me.

The dean hesitates. "Is there something else we should be discussing?" He looks over the top of my head, to my sister, I presume.

"No," I say, shooting up from my seat. "Of course not." Realizing I'm standing, I quickly sit back down. "I'm honored you thought of me, thank you." I blow out the air in my lungs.

"Coach Stephens will be there as well. We were hoping to have Coach Evans in attendance, but we know he'd be pleased with us asking you," Rebecca concludes.

"It's my pleasure. Um, Sir, may I ask where Coach Evans will be?" I ask the dean.

He looks to Rebecca then down at the schedule before him, picking up a pen. "We'll be making a formal announcement next week. Thank you for your time, Ms. Peters." *Formal announcement?*

I walk out of his office and past Brooke. We make eye contact but neither says a word. As I walk back to practice, I try sending Trey one more text.

Me: *Where are you? What is going on?*

I let a couple minutes go by. When he doesn't respond, I reenter the aquatic center, which now looks so empty without him.

Chapter Fifteen

My mom once told me that you can never find love too early. You don't want to miss an opportunity of a lifetime just because you thought you weren't ready for something so strong or powerful. I'm beginning to think that's not true. That maybe you can find it too early.

As I sit in the center of my bed with a bag of jalapeno potato chips and nothing but the glow from the TV dimly lighting my room, I wonder why people fall in love knowing it can cause heartache in the end.

"Knock, knock." There's a light tap on my door. Ali comes into view. "Can you talk?"

"Sure." I lean over and turn on my bedside lamp.

Ali's stick-straight hair fans up as she walks into my room and bounces on the bed next to me. "How you holding up? I haven't seen much of you." I bite the inside of my cheek. Giving her a small shrug, I stay silent. "I'm sorry, Emma. I know you're hurting."

"I'll be okay. Everything happens for a reason, right?" At least that's what I've been told. I'm not sure what the reason was for Trey to come into my life just to be taken away so quickly, but there has to be some unknown life lesson associated with him and this situation.

She reaches over and pats the top of my hand. Her eyes are gentle. "She'll come around. I know her."

Yeah, so do I. "I'm not so sure about that. She and I never fight. I honestly thought she went to the board today." I shake my head at the thought.

"Listen, I love your sister, but we both know how she can get sometimes. She was hurt when she said those words. I'm sure she's just as hurt and confused as you were when you learned who Trey was. She's the type of woman that falls hard, overreacts easily, but always accepts apologies within time. She'd never report you."

"Well, I'm not taking my chances, as much as it sucks. And with him gone this past week, I feel this aching void. I didn't get closure." I look up at her, my eyes beginning to gloss over. "I love him." I haven't said the words yet, which makes them seem like a foreign language to me. I'm not sure I've ever even been in love with a man. The word tends to get tossed around so easily among couples that I've never wanted to say the words to anyone until I felt it. I know I feel it with Trey, even with the big gap of success between us. When I described the feelings of being in the water to him, I know that's how I feel when I'm with him. He consumes my body. He makes me want to be one with him on so many levels, completing a part of me I didn't know needed to be complete.

Ali's body relaxes before me. "Em, falling in love isn't something you plan for. Love happens when it's meant to and it feels right. You don't get to choose it, and you can't force it. You're not supposed to. Don't be ashamed of falling in love with him."

"I didn't expect for this to happen. I miss him. I've gotten so used to him being a part of my life that I'm not sure I want him out of it."

"Then don't. Go to him. Be with him." Her eyes glimmer in the wavering light. "Only you know what feels right and what doesn't. With everything in life also come risks. If he's worth it, you'll know and then there's no reason to deny it."

"He's gone. I don't know where he is and the dean wouldn't tell me. I think Brooke scared him off."

"She'll come to her senses sooner or later. The hopeless romantic she is won't be able to deny you your happiness. If you and Trey love each other like you say, then there's no reason you shouldn't be together."

"But there's always the issue of him going back to Michigan in the spring."

"And there will be more obstacles thrown

your way. You're twenty years old, with a full life ahead of you. Don't let love pass you by because you're too scared of an outcome you don't even know yet."

"She's right," Brooke's voice breaks through. She's standing in my bedroom doorway, hands on each side of the wooden doorframe. Her eyes are somber as she listens in on our conversation. "May I?" she asks, seeking permission before stepping further.

"Yes."

"Emma, I didn't know you two were that serious. I thought it was just a fling. I didn't want to hear it when I saw you two and listening to you now makes me feel like the world's shittiest sister." She sits down in my computer chair, across from my bed.

"You're not a shitty sister, Brooke." My voice is low. "You just didn't want to listen."

"You took me by surprise. I've met one boyfriend of yours, and that was at least three years ago. I never expected that, the next time I saw you with one, he'd be the guy I briefly dated. Let alone..."

"I know, I know." I sit up taller. "It wasn't like I went out looking to fall in love with my swim coach. You have to know that I never wanted to hurt you, but I owed it to myself to see what the feelings I had for him meant."

She licks her lips, nodding. "I know. I was shocked. Hell, I'm still shocked. Do you two know how much trouble you could have gotten into if you were caught by someone else?"

"He's worth the risk." I say it again in my head. My eyes drift to Ali's. She gives me an understanding smile.

"I'm going to leave you two alone," Ali says as she stands up. Her hand gives mine a tight squeeze before leaving Brooke and I alone.

"Brooke, listen. I love him, and I was..."

She stops me. "Emma, I won't tell anyone. I wouldn't do that to you. When I saw you coming into the office today I swear I lost my breath. I was so nervous that someone found out and you were going to get in trouble and lose your scholarship. I would never do that to you. I said those words to be spiteful. I was hurt and mad and I wanted to hurt him more than I wanted to hurt you. And for that, I'm sorry. I was stunned. I really liked Trey, but when I look back now I agree with him. We were better off as friends. I was foolish to say what I did. It was heated." She stands up and walks over to the bed, sitting next to me. I rest my head on her shoulder, and she curves her arm around my waist.

"I need you to know I would never do anything to hurt you, Brooke. When I was with him it was like no one else mattered but us. That may sound selfish, and hell, what we were doing was selfish, because we weren't thinking of anyone but us." I know this next part may be hard for her to hear, but I continue. "There's an undeniable chemistry between us. I believe in lust at first sight, not love, but when we first met we connected on a level I never knew existed. Yes, there's a physical attraction, but we have this magnetic pull to one another. We share so many of the same passions that I'm not sure I'll ever meet anyone like him. Keeping our relationship a secret was to protect everyone involved."

Her eyes become red as she rubs the tears away. "Then you need to see where that path takes you, Emma."

"I'm scared that it might be too late."

She rubs her nose. "What do you mean?"

My face falls. I will the tears away. My heart aches at the thought of him telling me he's letting me go.

"He said he was letting me go."

"But is a future without each other better?"

It's not. There's no life without love and happiness. I'll always have swimming. That's inevitable. It's who I am and what I was born to do. But I'll never have another Trey Evans.

Chapter Sixteen

The wind blows through the Saturday morning air. I rush into the school with Erin and the other teammates. From the sounds of cheers and clapping coming from inside the aquatic center one would imagine half the student body is here.

Entering the locker room, the smell of various fragrances mixed together causes my nose to scrunch upward. Deodorant bottles rest along the ledge of a large mirror that's hanging on a wall that separates the large room into two. Swim caps are laid out in a variety of vibrant colors on the gray tile floor, making it look like a large game of Twister.

I head over to my locker, spinning the combo wheel to open it. My swimsuit is hanging neatly inside along with my goggles and two caps. Flip-flops snap against the wet floor as one of my teammates walks by. She gives a wave before heading out to the pool.

Once I'm changed into windbreaker pants over my suit, I close my locker and see Erin walking over.

"You ready?" She arches a brow.

"Yeah." Stretching my arms out behind me, I welcome the pull to my muscles. "I need to loosen up first." My individual free-style is up shortly, with the 4x100 medley shortly after.

I leave the locker room and enter the pool area to find the bleachers filled with students, family members, faculty, and people from the community. The view brings a tender smile to my face. Brooke and Ali are sitting front and center next to my parents. I give them a giant smile and wave.

I spot my team off to the left, watching the fifty-meter backstroke competitors. As I continue to scan the area I find Trey standing next to Coach Johnson. They're deep in conversation with the officials.

My temperature rises at the sight of him. My mouth twists upward as I hold my breath. *He's here.* He's gorgeous, but looks just as tired as I do. There are faint bags under his eyes, small lines crease around his eyes, and his hair is disheveled, like he's run his hands through it twenty times. By the way he looks I can tell he hasn't slept at all this week, just like me. His posture appears anything but relaxed in his jeans and Bentwood University Swimming polo shirt.

The second I take a step forward, his head shoots up in my direction. He meets me halfway. I can't read his face. It's a cross between torture and excitement.

"I didn't think you were going to be here," I declare. The corners of my mouth begin to lift.

His eyes seep into mine. "How are you? You doing okay?" His fingers slide into his pockets and his head dips down slightly. He looks shy.

"Trey Evans, are you blushing?" There's a hint of laughter to my voice, trying my best to make a joke. I hate awkwardness.

He runs his fingers across his chin, studying me. "Emma..." He trails off.

I know he's not asking if I'm prepared for my race. I long to reach up and take his face between my hands, and it takes everything inside of me to refrain. Looking over at Coach Johnson, who is walking over and watching us, I reply quickly, "I'm relieved. I'm doing much better now that you-"

"Fantastic." There's a bite to his tone. "I'm glad to hear you're doing so well. Why don't you head on over and stretch—you'll be up soon." His eyes become distant as he looks away.

"Trey?" I need him to look at me. I need him to see that what I'm feeling inside is yearning for the need to be close to him. That I crave to hold his hand, kiss him and tell him I love him. That I'm relieved to see him.

"It's Coach Evans here, Emma," he sneers. He looks past me and walks away, leaving my heart to sink just a little. Coach Johnson doesn't say a word as he comes to stand next to me, but I can see the puzzlement spinning in his head.

"Excuse me Coach Johnson." I give an apologetic smile and follow after Trey.

"What's going on, Trey?" I need answers. "Why are you so angry with me?"

He stops. I take that as my cue to get in front of him. "You're relieved? And doing much better?"

"If you wouldn't have interrupted me you would have heard what I was trying to say."

"I'm fucking crushed," he whispers forcefully.

I use the same tone right back at him. "*You're* crushed? I've tried to reach you so many times! You won't call me back! *You're* the one that went running when the times got tough."

"To protect you!" His voice is a little louder, causing my body to jerk. His nostrils flare.

Coach Johnson walks up. "You're in lane four, Emma."

"Thanks." My smile barely lifts.

I turn to move. Trey snatches my wrist and whispers, "Look, I'm still your coach, and I need you to be in the zone right now. I can't have you being pissed off when you have a race to swim.

So, please go out..."

"Being pissed just feeds the adrenaline. This isn't over, *Coach*." With my right hand, I clamp down onto his hand and pry it loose.

Getting into my lane, I take off my windbreaker pants. Coach Johnson walks up and takes them from me. He hands me my goggles and I slip them over my cap. This is what I live for. The rush. The way the adrenaline skates through my muscles, heightening my senses, and expanding my heart so my blood pumps faster. I get on my knees and lean into the pool, cupping water in my palms and splash it over my face. I do one last stretch and shake it out. I catch a glimpse of Trey off to the side. His mouth is straight, his face expressionless. Coach Johnson is toward the center of the pool, where I know I can always count on him to be. He likes to chant words of encouragement to us, even though he knows we're zoning everything out, but I still enjoy his shadow watching above.

As soon as the buzzer goes off, we all dive downward into the warm water. Like I've done so many times before, I push and move my body through the water with so much force. With each stroke my body becomes weightless. I slither through the blue thickness. Rumbles from the chanting and stomping vibrate through my chest as I push myself harder. Filling my lungs, I hold the hot breath of air, darting underneath the water to make my turn. I can see someone to my right out of the corner of my eye. Tossing any thoughts or worries aside, I come up to the surface and blow out the air. My head dips into the water, arms and legs slicing through the thickness. With each breath I move my head to the opposite side. When I don't think I'm kicking or moving hard enough, I push myself faster. The second I touch the wall, I rip the goggles from my face, panting to look at the time board. My eyes blur from the droplets of water in my lashes, but I can see my name flashing in bold red letters next to "1" with a time of 52.04. I slam my fists into the water with excitement.

My eyes look around to find Trey. He takes a few long strides in my direction with a look of admiration spread across his face. He offers his hand to me, and I take it. With ease, he withdraws my body from the water. My nose tips up to get a better look. His lips beg to be touched, but his body tells me differently, as he holds me an arm's length away.

"Excuse me," he mutters under his breath.

"Where you going, Coach?" Erin asks, all smiles.

"You guys celebrate. I'll be right back."

I watch as he walks away. Before I even know what I'm doing, I step away from the team and grab my flip-flops and pants to run after him.

Chapter Seventeen

"Trey!" I call his name as I push open the main doors. The wind blows into my damp hair, causing it to stick to my cheek. A light shudder slides down my arms.

I spot him in the parking lot next to his SUV. I start to run when he begins to open his door. I scream his name.

He looks up, perturbed. "Emma? What are you doing?"

"I don't care about the repercussions. I choose you," I say. "I want to be with you." I rush the words out, afraid if I don't get them out now I never will. "This past week has been torture."

Desperate eyes stare back at me. "Emma, I can't do this."

"Well, I can." I step into the open door so I'm blocking his way. "I need you to believe in us, because I do. You said when we started this journey that it's you and me. I will burn with you, Trey Evans. Whatever comes of this, I'll be right there with you. I'm not ready to let you go. I love you."

He steps back, stunned. "What?"

"I'm not willing to let you go."

"No, the other part." His lips begin to twitch.

I smile. "I love you."

He takes a small step to close the distance between us. Brushing the hair off my face, he looks down at me. "Say it again."

"I love you." I stand on my tiptoes and kiss his chin. "I want to be with you, Trey. I'm tired of keeping this a secret and I'm tired of being afraid. I want to hold your hand as we walk down the street, kiss you on the sidewalk, and share every hope and dream of mine with you. You're all I've been able to think about this past week, and I can't bear another moment without you. I don't care what happens, as long as you're by my side."

His eyes shift to the front doors. "I quit this week."

My heart stops. "What?"

He looks back at me and lets out a long exhale. I step back, but his hand snatches my wrist. "I can't do this, Emma." Tears pour into my eyes. My heart feels like it's splitting all over again. "I interviewed for another coaching position for next year."

I try to push out of his hold, but his grip tightens. "In Miami."

I stop fighting. My eyes dart to his. "You're staying?"

I can feel his heart racing. The vein on the side of his neck throbs. I'm all ears as I wait for him to talk.

"Emma, when I said I was letting you go because I care, that was the truth, but it's also because I care that I couldn't bear to be away from you. After you walked out of my office, I knew there was no way I'd ever be able to go back to Michigan. I told the administration I had some personal things come up and this would be my last race. Coach Johnson will shift into the head coaching position. I won't know about the job for at least another couple weeks, but I won't stop until I find something here. In Florida. I don't know where our future will lead us, but I do know I want you by my side, wherever it goes. Starting now."

I crash my lips to his, twisting my fingers in his hair. He cries out into my mouth, his breath warm against my lips.

Our pace slows and eventually comes to an end. He wraps his hands around my waist. Every nerve ending in my body shrieks with the simplest of touches. "You better get inside, you have another race to do and I'm still your coach for another two hours."

I giggle. "I'm going to miss calling you that."

His eyes grow large. "I'm always up for role playing."

My smile matches his liveliness.

"Come on, let's get another win under your belt so I can take you back to my place and congratulate you properly."

We drive up to Trey's house in silence. I feel as if we've come full circle, ending up at the place where we first met. It's the perfect start to our new beginning. He gets out from behind the wheel all too eagerly. He laces our fingers, leading the way up the newly painted steps to his place.

He picks me up and carries me into the house.

"Bed. Now," I order against his chest.

He moves with ease up the steps and into his room, where he places me back down on the floor. In one swift motion, Trey's in front of me taking off my shirt and unclasping my bra. My nipples are firm and erect. He rolls them between his fingers. His cool breath against my stiff nipple explodes the current inside of me.

"Like that," I moan.

His hands squeeze my breasts, filling his palms. "God, I missed you."

I welcome the gentle twinge of pain. My head falls back, enjoying his hands caressing my body. I can't say for sure how long he plays with my breasts, but as our hearts continue to beat the passing seconds away, I feel his cock becoming erect against my inner thigh.

We walk together with our mouths connected and hands exploring one another. He removes my pants and kicks them aside. I slide out of my thong, letting my body be free before him.

"Fuck, you are the sexiest woman." His warm mouth covers my neck. A delicious shudder warms my body.

I give his hair a gentle tug. "I need you inside of me, Trey."

The ache grows.

He growls.

Standing straight, he tears off his clothing. His eyes flare, causing my stomach to flip. Locking my mouth to his chest, I swirl my tongue along his flesh and over to his nipple, massaging it.

"Don't torture me," he hisses.

I laugh against him.

Trey takes hold of my body and takes me over to the bed. He flips me so I'm resting on my hands and knees, bare ass hanging in the air. He gives it a smack, making me cry out in inclination. His palms press against the backs of my knees, spreading my legs further apart, and then he lays his palms on my hips, his erection poking at my slit. I twinge with joy as my core becomes wet. Trey's fingers run along my slick folds. I look back and watch him rub it along his thick cock.

"Take me," I breathe. His cock rests at my entrance, taunting me. "Trey!" I beg. He slowly eases his way in.

His movements are slow at first, gentle even. When I push back against him, he begins to pick up the pace, his balls slapping loud against my clit. I cry out louder. My insides pulse, clamping tighter around him. He continues to rock in and out of me.

"Yes," I rush out. "Fill me."

He balls my hair up into his fist and tugs. His left hand digs into my flesh as he continues to sink in and out me, hard. Moaning, I look over my shoulder to watch. He spanks my bare cheek and then abruptly stops, withdrawing himself.

"Ride me," he pants, switching positions. I do as I'm told. Once he's flat against the bed, I straddle his hips and slowly impale myself down on his shaft. As he fills me, my eyes flutter shut. Trey hisses under his breath as he sweeps the hair off my shoulders, exposing my neck.

Sitting up so we're chest to chest, he whispers in my ear, "Do you like that, Emma?"

"God, yes," I breathe.

"Show me what you like." His hands rest on my hips as I rock against him. "I've never been more turned on in my life," he grunts.

My hands claim his chest, tracing the outline of his pectoral muscles.

"That's it," he says. "Cling to my dick."

I moan out from the pure pleasure of him fulfilling me. His thumb rubs fast circles over my clit and my body begins to vibrate against him. His hands run through my hair, tilting my head backward so he can kiss my neck.

"I'm so close," I pant. I tilt my head to kiss Trey with everything I have. Shivers of delight spread over me as heat floods my body.

"Take it. Ride me, baby." I begin to pump his cock faster. I can feel his smile against my mouth. His warm breath sends sweet twinges of ecstasy down my spine. My body is sheening with sweat as passion continues to inch through my veins. Trey gives my shoulder a few soft kisses, transporting my body to the clouds as I break out with pleasure. He follows, erupting inside of me. We cling to one another, unable to move. There are no sounds except for our heavy breathing. His body glistens with sweat. Sliding off him and nestling myself into his side, I bunch his comforter up to our chests.

"I'm not letting you go. You know that, right?" Trey says in a husky, lingering tone.

My lips brush against his neck. "I'd be disappointed if you did."

People experience love differently and at different points in their life. True love holds no limits.

And for anyone who's lucky enough to experience it, I say embrace it. It's the best feeling in the world.

Acknowledgements

A special thanks to my readers. You all are some of the best readers in the world, and I don't know what I did to deserve you. Thank you for your support, emails, Facebook messages, tweets, and coming out to see me at signings. I appreciate you reading and falling in love with the stories I create. My heart is filled with so much love for you. As always, this book is for you.

A big thank-you to my writing partner in crime, Brooke. You (almost) always answer my calls and politely listen as I endlessly talk out my ideas. Thank you for encouraging me to write. You're an amazing writer and an even better friend. Even though you choose to live over 500 miles away from me, I can't imagine going on this journey without you. Thank you for bringing the words back.

This book would be nowhere if it weren't for Kosta and the entire Vasko and Creative Online Publishing team. I'm so blessed to be surrounded by such an amazing support system. Thank you, Kosta, for giving me this opportunity, believing in my words, and allowing me to write what I love. I'm looking forward to many more books and years with you.

To all the bloggers who have shared my books over the years: Thank you for reviewing and being involved with this beautiful book community. Each one of you is so crucial. I'm grateful for all your hard work and the time you put into your love of books.

And lastly, to my family. Thank you for letting me sneak off to write. You mean the world to me. I love you to the stars and back.

About the Author

Amanda Maxlyn is a *USA Today* bestselling author who writes contemporary and new adult romance. She craves creating powerful and emotional stories while weaving in a good mix of steamy and sexy passion. Books are meant to make us feel and expect the unexpected. As a writer, Amanda believes words should make you bleed with emotion, and she hopes to bring readers out of their comfort zones while also sending them on an unforgettable journey that will stay with them forever. She's not afraid to push the limits and thinks you shouldn't be either.

To stay updated on current information and upcoming novels, make sure to visit her at:

www.amandamaxlyn.com

Made in the USA
Lexington, KY
13 April 2017